The Chief's Proposal

by

Sandra Dailey

The Chief's Proposal

Cover Art by *Debby Taylor*

The Wild Rose Press, Inc.
PO Box 708
Adams Basin, NY 14410-0708
Visit us at www.thewildrosepress.com

Publishing History
First Champagne Rose Edition, 2012
Digital ISBN 978-1-61217-325-2
Print ISBN 978-1-62830-419-0

Published in the United States of America

"Why do we need a fire?" Ginny asked.

"We need all the elements." Brett motioned toward the lake, the sky, the ground, and back to the fire as he said, "Water, air, earth and fire."

"Is this a Native American thing?"

Brett lowered his head and shook it. It was becoming a gesture she recognized as him gathering patience. He did it a lot around her.

"Yeah, in your language this would be called a truth telling."

"What would your people call it?"

"A truth telling. Now will you pay attention?" Brett stretched out on the blanket with his head resting on his saddle. "Come down here and make yourself comfortable."

Ginny copied his pose, and then asked, "What's next?"

"I'm going to ask you a question and you have to answer it, honestly and completely. After that, I'll answer a question you have. What is said will stay here when we leave."

"What's your question?"

Brett turned his head to look at her. She'd never seen him look so serious.

"Why is it such a bad thing to be married to me? I know I'm no prize, but you look as if you've just received a death sentence."

Ginny thought for a long moment. "I don't know if it will be bad. I don't really know you. I just hadn't imagined myself being married to anyone, ever."

Dedication

This book is dedicated to my mother
for her constant support,
assistance, and encouragement.
And
a big thank you to Cindy Davis,
the editor who never sleeps.

Chapter One

"911, what's your emergency?"

Ginny Dearing wiped blood from above her left eye. "I've had a car accident. I'm on the county road between I-75 and Three Trees, Georgia. My car is stuck in a ditch and my doors are blocked. I can't get out."

Ginny tried to sound calm, but she was terrified. Being from Saginaw, Michigan, she'd never seen a swamp much less driven through one. She had no idea what kind of creatures lurked right outside her doors. But the one creature she dreaded most tonight was the man who had sent for her—Brett Silverfeather—her fiancé, a man she'd never laid eyes on. Could this possibly be worth the job she'd been promised?

After answering questions for the emergency operator for fifteen minutes, blue lights flashed overhead and the whine of sirens could be heard approaching. She was finally able to end the call. In moments, a tall, thin man climbed down to her. He was an EMT. Suddenly, her rescuer lost his footing in the slick red clay and slid into her car door with a solid thud.

"Jeez-o-Pete," the man exclaimed, "this clay is slicker 'n snot."

Another voice called from above. "Best call Bernie and let him know he'll need more equipment to get this little buggy outta here."

A third man laughed. "Knowing Bernie, he'll just crawl on down there and toss that thing back up on the road." Everyone laughed with him but Ginny.

1

The man by her door squinted as he looked her over. "Where'd ya get hurt ma'am?"

"I'm fine except for this bump on my head." Ginny lifted her bangs to show him the bleeding spot near her hairline.

The EMT sucked air between his teeth as he peered at the wound. "Okay, well, that's gonna leave a mark, but it don't look too bad. Shed your shoes. I'll pull you through the window and help you climb up outta here."

Ginny hesitated. This rescue certainly wasn't like any she'd seen on TV. By the time she'd clumsily scaled the slimy wall, she was covered in red Georgia clay.

At the roadside, she found there were actually four men present. Two were wearing white EMT shirts and the other two were dressed in green county uniforms. Behind the ambulance was a standard patrol car.

The second EMT helped her inside and sat her on a folded gurney while he sat on a bench opposite her.

"The names Lucas Barns, ma'am," Lucas looked at her forehead and grimaced. "I don't think you'll need stitches, but you're sure gonna have one heck of a shiner come mornin'."

"Would that be your professional opinion, Lucas?" Ginny asked with a grin. As the new high school English teacher, she finally felt she'd come to the right place.

"Yes sir-e-bob," he answered as he twisted and shook an ice pack. He placed it over her forehead. "This'll keep the swellin' down."

The icy plastic bag felt so wonderful in the heat, Ginny wished she had one under each armpit. However, she was willing to settle for a hotel room with a shower and clean sheets.

The penlight flashing in front of her eyes didn't

help the pain in Ginny's head. Neither did the shrill whistle from one of the deputies outside.

"This here car's got Michigan plates on it," The whistler shouted.

The first EMT wiped his muddy hands on a blue shop towel. "So what?"

"So, the chief has been waitin' for a woman from Michigan since early mornin'." The deputy ran to the open doors of the ambulance and looked in at Ginny with owlish eyes. "Are you Ms. Dearing, ma'am?"

Ginny hesitated, "Yes I am."

"Holy crap," The deputy raced back to his car. He spoke into his two-way radio for a moment and then returned. "You boys'd better get her over to the clinic in Three Trees, pronto."

Lucas rolled his eyes. "Where's the fire, Carl? Her injuries ain't critical."

Carl had already run back to the radio in his car, but the second deputy answered for him. "Hear tell, the chief was all in knots this mornin' and by lunchtime he was purely pissed. By the time he left for the house, he was mad as all get-out. Who you've got here is the new schoolteacher. And she's the chief's woman, Ms. Dearing is."

Ginny smiled nervously when both EMTs turned to stare at her. "Please, just call me Ginny," she said.

Lucas asked the deputy, "Does he know how small and...well...pale she is?"

"Well, I'd guess so, dipstick. He's plannin' on marryin' her," the deputy said over his shoulder as he ran after his partner.

The first EMT jumped behind the wheel of the ambulance and started the engine. "Tommy Lane, at your service, Ms. Dearing."

Even though she'd been rescued, Ginny was still shook up. She needed to relax and stop worrying about what waited down the road. The least of which being the deer that had run in front of her car. She positioned herself to watch out the front windshield of the ambulance.

Her first impression of nightlife in Three Trees was that it looked like an old western ghost town. Along the curbs were streetlights, but they were the old fashioned type, six-foot black iron posts with lantern like tops. Small storefronts along the four blocks of Main Street were dark. A grassy median in the center of the street boasted three huge oak trees. Ginny assumed they were the explanation for the town's name.

At the end of this mini-metropolis, they made a left turn and parked in the circular drive of a large Victorian house. A sign hanging over the front steps of the porch read, Three Trees Medical Clinic. The windows were dark here as well.

After three rings of the doorbell, they were greeted by a middle-aged couple wearing pajamas and robes.

"What's the problem here?" the man asked.

"Car accident out on the north county road," Lucas answered. He added in an ominous tone, "This here is the chief's woman, Ms. Virginia Dearing."

"Didn't know the chief had a woman," the lady said as she smiled and held her hand out to Ginny. "I'm Nora Baxter and this is my husband, Doctor Jack Baxter. I don't recall seeing you around town."

"I've just come from Saginaw, Michigan. I wish you'd call me Ginny." She shook Nora's hand.

The doctor smiled kindly at Ginny and then spoke to his wife. "Better get here into the treatment room, Nora, so I can look her over."

The waiting room inside the clinic looked like an old-fashioned tea parlor, but the treatment rooms were as modern as any you'd find in the city. Ginny sat on the end of an examination table while Nora gently washed the blood from the side of her face.

"Nora, I have a question."

4

"What's that, darlin'?"

Ginny hesitated, "Why does everyone seem so afraid of Brett Silverfeather? Is he really as bad as they make him out to be?"

Nora looked thoughtful for a moment. "Well, I once heard someone describe the sheriff as being as mean as a bear with a bad haircut. He doesn't put up with anybody breaking the law and he expects the best from his deputies. He's a little stubborn and short on patience, but I've never known of him mistreatin' anybody, man or animal. Of course I shouldn't have to tell you 'bout that, but you've probably only seen his softer side."

Ginny simply smiled agreeably and nodded. She could already see that Nora would make a good friend. She didn't want to spoil their rapport by admitting she'd never laid eyes on her future husband.

When Nora opened the door to leave the room, Ginny could see her four rescuers plus a newcomer. Her heart nearly stopped at the sight of the stranger.

The man stood with his back to Ginny glaring down at the deputies and EMTs. He was also dressed in a green uniform. He was at least 6'4", which seemed huge to a 5'4" woman. His wide shoulders and broad back were dissected by a long black braid that nearly touched his narrow waist. Fists at the ends of dark muscular arms rested on a thick black gun belt. It held a real gun, a big one. His deep, rumbling voice sent vibrations through every nerve in her body.

"I have a mind to sandpaper your heads bald," the stranger said sternly. "Just tell me which one of you yahoos called your woman while you were responding to an emergency call?"

Carl must have been the bravest of the four men because he was the one who answered. "The only person we talked to all night was Pam."

"Pam, I should have known," the man growled, when he heard his dispatcher's name. "Pamela Armstrong, aka the mouth of the south, has the phone lines buzzing all over town. I don't want any of you talking about other people's business. Understood? You know how I feel about gossip."

Ginny made a choking sound. She was already the subject of gossip? It was after midnight and she hadn't seen anyone who wasn't still waiting outside her door.

The man stopped his tirade when he heard the sound behind him. He swung around and faced her with a scowl. His skin was smooth and dark over high cheekbones, a strong jawline, and a long thin nose. He was, without a doubt, the most beautiful, yet masculine, man she'd ever seen. He nearly scared the life right out of her.

His cat-like amber eyes widened with astonishment as they scanned her appearance. He bowed his head and gave it a slow shake. On his chest was a sheriff's badge over one breast pocket and a nameplate that read Silverfeather over the other. This man was her future husband.

Ginny slammed the door. Holy smoke he was huge, handsome, and had the personality of Attila the Hun.

Suddenly she wondered what kind of impression she'd made on him. Ginny looked down and groaned. Her best blouse and jeans had been smeared with clay and blood. She looked about as appealing as a bag lady, except that she didn't have shoes on. Even bag ladies didn't run around without something on their feet.

Ginny spotted a small mirror mounted on the wall over the sink. She rushed over to look at her face and nearly fainted. Her chin length blonde hair was in damp strings, rust colored by clay, and she had a purplish welt that covered the left side of her forehead from the center of her brow to her temple. It looked as bright as a neon sign against her pale skin. She tugged on her wispy bangs, but there was no way to hide it. This would need a lot more than Max Factor. This required spackle and three coats of enamel based paint, the exterior kind.

Ginny was curled in a ball in the corner, wishing herself back to Michigan, when the doctor walked into the room.

Dr. Baxter coaxed her to the examining table to look her over. Afterward, he got up to wash his hands and give his diagnosis. "Well, Missy, if you keep that cut clean it should heal nicely. You've got a heck of a bruise, but the ice pack helped a lot. Luckily, the impact wasn't in an area that would affect your eye. If you need to take something for pain or stiffness, a couple of ibuprofen will be fine. If you have any other problems, you can call me anytime. All in all, you're a very lucky girl."

"Doctor, I don't have any insurance, but I've got a little cash," Ginny said meekly. What she had was the last three hundred dollars to her name and it was in her purse somewhere in the swamp.

"No need for that," the doctor groused. "I've been treating the chief ever since he returned home from college and pinned on a deputy badge. Believe me, he and his clan have given me more business than any man has a right to. Luckily, I didn't have to use more than a Band-Aid this time."

Ginny knew he wasn't exactly telling the truth. It had cost him a decent night's sleep. Tonight, she was well aware of how valuable sleep was and she was grateful.

Now, she could find a ride to a hotel and get cleaned up and rested. All she had to do was bypass the incredible hulk in the waiting room.

She opened the door very slowly and peeked

around it. Instead of the sheriff, the two deputies waited for her on the other side. They both stood when she entered the waiting room.

The husky man with blonde hair spoke first. "My name is Carl Sights, ma'am. I hope you're feelin' better." He indicated the small redheaded deputy beside him. "This here is Larry Graham. He got all your things out of your car. Larry, don't talk a whole lot, but he's as wiry and nimble as a spider monkey. He climbed right on in there."

Larry held out her purse and shoes. "Nice to meet ya, ma'am. The chief is bringin' his car up to the door to collect you."

Ginny wondered if there was a back door she could get to, quickly.

The deputies said goodnight to her, the doctor, and Nora, before excusing themselves to return to work. The doctor also said goodnight and climbed the stairs to his bedroom. Ginny waited for them all to leave, and then asked Nora a question that had been needling her since she arrived.

"Nora, of all the people I've met tonight, you're the only one who offered to shake my hand. I know I don't look very presentable at the moment, but I'm basically a nice person. Am I missing something here? Have I done something to offend them?"

Nora chuckled, "Welcome to small town southern manners, hun. A man don't touch a lady without her invitation. Did you see the way those boys stood up when you came in the room? You can really use that one if you ever have a mind to pester 'em. Just make a lot of trips in and out. They'll be going up and down like a bunch of jumping beans.

"Our men are a special breed. It's ingrained in 'em from birth. They show respect to their women folk. Their momma's would have their hides nailed to the barn door otherwise. That is, the ones who were raised up right, like the chief and his boys. But don't you worry. You'll do just fine. It'll just take a little time to get used to our ways."

Ginny stored the information in her mental files. She would have a lot to get used to. That is, if neither she nor Brett Silverfeather backed out of their agreement. Just the thought of him sent a shiver down her spine. She wasn't sure if it was caused by fear or physical attraction. She'd had a strong reaction to him in both ways. Neither one was good. She needed to keep both reactions suppressed if this was going to work. She'd come to Three Trees for only one purpose, and that purpose was to teach.

The door opened and Brett Silverfeather walked back inside. He looked back and forth between Ginny and Nora a few times. Ginny couldn't be sure, but his complexion seemed to be turning a little redder.

"Guess we'd better be getting home now. You have a good night, Miss Nora," he said.

Nora appeared to be amused by his embarrassment. She raised an eyebrow and gave Brett a sly smile. "You have a good night too, Chief."

Brett reddened more, cleared his throat, and followed Ginny outside where he tossed her two large suitcases into the back of his SUV as if they were feather pillows. She happened to know they weighed a ton. Next he pulled out a small blanket to cover the passenger seat. Then he stood by the door staring at her, arms folded, muscles bulging. She wasn't sure she wanted to get within ten feet of him. She stood her ground, staring back.

After a long moment he asked, "Do you need help getting in? I was told you weren't badly injured."

Ginny pictured him picking her up and tossing her into the cargo space with the bags. She gave up, got in, and he shut the door. Claustrophobia slid over her like a stinky, wet blanket.

The silence made her edgy as they drove away from town. "You know, I could just get a hotel room. It wasn't my intention to impose..."

"Why?" When she didn't answer he added, "If you're thinking what I think you are, you can relax. I'm dog tired and you're, well...not exactly in top form either."

Ginny couldn't help but wonder what might happen the next night and the nights after that one. They hadn't discussed sleeping arrangements and such in their e-mails. He was definitely gorgeous, but she wasn't sure about his character. If he handled his women the way he did his deputies she wasn't sure she wanted anything to do with him. She'd known men like him before and their relationships had never ended well. Furthermore, just because he was her fiancé didn't negate the fact that they'd just met moments ago. They hadn't even had their first conversation yet.

"You know, you could have called," Brett blurted. "I expected you to be here early this morning. I didn't know if you'd had an accident and died on the side of the road or just changed your mind and stayed up north."

Ginny wished she'd done either one at that particular moment. She crossed her arms tightly over her chest and slouched slightly. "I didn't have your number."

"You knew I worked for the sheriff's department. You could have called the office at any time. What held you up for so long—sightseeing, souvenir shopping, or mountain climbing?"

Ginny's temper rose to a bubbling boil. "You have no idea what I've been through in the last forty-one hours. This was supposed to be a leisurely drive down I-75. My route was supposed to practically take me from my front door to yours.

"Instead, I've driven through monsoons in four

10

different states. There were nothing but eighteen-wheelers and RVs around me, throwing water over my windshield. It was like being the marble in a pinball machine, a wet and foggy pinball machine.

"The number of accidents was incredible. I spent hours just sitting still. It's a good thing there was nothing to drink because there were also no bathrooms. I pictured myself turning into a big, dried up piece of jerky." She stopped for a breath.

"I was only detoured off the interstate four times, which believe it or not, was lucky. I lost count of the construction sites at twelve. That was when one of my tires blew out.

"At that point, I decided to stop for the night. I'd intended to get a nice hot shower and a good night's sleep. Do you want to know what I got instead? A shower in a tub, with what I hope was rust in the bottom, which only gave lukewarm water. And, a bar next door that featured a very loud band until four in the morning. Is that even legal? There was a neon sign outside flashing Redneck Rendezvous...all night long.

"I started back out this morning at the crack of dawn. The only thing to eat for miles was stale donuts and acid based coffee. Where's all that great southern cuisine I always hear about?" Another breath.

"Do you want to know how my day was today? I drove through more rain, huge vehicles, accidents, and construction sites. The only difference, it was even hotter. For Heaven's sake, is this Georgia or did I take a wrong turn into hell? My car doesn't have air conditioning, that's right, no air. And, my radio is broken, no tunes either."

Ginny threw her head back against the seat and closed her eyes. "I should have asked the doctor for a tetanus shot and a valium."

Brett was impressed. She had barely taken a

breath. She might have broken his record for endurance in the tantrums and tirades category. He turned to her and said, "You still could have called."

So, that was their first conversation. Ginny saw her life going south in more ways than one.

After another long stretch of silence, she asked, "Can I turn on the siren?"

"No."

"The lights?"

"No."

"The radio?"

"No. Rule number two. Don't touch anything in the county car."

"You're no fun at all," Ginny pouted.

"I'm never fun when I'm in uniform."

"What about when you're out of uniform?" Ginny realized what she'd said and quickly glanced his way. Brett watched the road with his lips tightly holding back a grin. She wondered what his smile would look like...or what he'd look like out of uniform. Dammit, he'd planted a seed in her mind that was already taking root and sprouting. She definitely needed some sleep.

The ride turned silent again before Ginny asked, "What's rule number one?"

He growled with exasperation before he said, "Show up on time, otherwise call me."

Chapter Two

Ginny had a feeling she'd made a big mistake, but what could she do. She'd passed the point of no return before she'd even started the trip. On Friday she'd collected her last check from the Stop-n-Shop convenience store. Early Saturday morning, she'd turned in the keys to her rented room.

Ginny looked out the window and forced each muscle in her body to relax. The road ahead was empty and quiet. It was the last leg of her journey to a new life. She intended to make the most of the situation. Whether it led to riches or ruin, Three Trees, Georgia, was her destiny. It had to be. It was the only option she had left.

After working so hard to get her teaching degree, Ginny had spent the last year at minimum wage jobs. She'd been desperate to find a teaching position. So desperate, in fact, she'd e-mailed her resume to every school board in the state of Michigan and all the surrounding states. Her intention was to keep widening her search until something panned out. Each week, she added another state. Finally the search had widened about as far as it could go, all the way across the continental United States.

Word of her job search spread to the local newspaper through a friend of hers who worked there. To her amazement, a financial specialist who'd read the article, mentioned it on the Good Morning Michigan show. They'd been discussing the innovative methods people were using to find jobs. A few weeks later, her search was featured in a story on the internet. Everyone admired her spunk, but she'd quickly found out it took more than spunk to find work in today's economy.

The year had gone by with no serious responses before the first e-mail arrived from Brett Silverfeather.

Ms. Virginia Dearing,

I am a leader in a small community in Georgia. I have ties to the school board with whom I've shared your story. We have a position opening in our High School this fall. The job does come with a few added responsibilities, which I would discuss with the right person.

Please reply with a copy of your resume and a short bio about yourself.

Brett Silverfeather

That e-mail had been the catalyst that had started this whole mess and eventually led her to Three Trees, Georgia.

Ginny pulled away from her thoughts to look out the window. Southern Georgia was kind of spooky late at night. Of course, it may have been because she was used to well-lit, city streets. The lonely country road was narrow with trees close on both sides. The SUVs high beams glowed on creepy moss hanging from gnarled looking trees. There wasn't another car in sight. The only indication of human life was an old wooden sign that read, U-pick Pecans. There was an event she'd be sure to avoid. Pecans should come from pastries and pretty nut dishes, not falling from nasty looking trees.

It suddenly occurred to her that the steady hum of the road had been replaced by a louder, more disturbing noise. The local wildlife was coming alive all around them. The sound of frogs and insects was almost deafening. She wondered if South Georgia had alligators and snakes, maybe even bears and wild cats. Between the animals outside and the man sitting next to her, Ginny felt about as safe as a turtle crossing a crowded highway.

More research might have been a good idea. Maybe she'd let her eagerness to start the new job take her too far. She hadn't even Googled Three Trees, Georgia. All she'd allowed herself to think about were textbooks, supplies, and lesson plans. She didn't want to think about the marriage she was blindly walking into. She knew she'd chicken out if she did.

Already her life had made a drastic change. She'd left home and friends behind, amidst cheers and well wishes for the new job. She hadn't told a single person what she agreed to do in order to get the job. If she ended up shackled to a wall in the sheriff's basement or at the business end of his chainsaw, no one would ever know.

Finally they turned into the driveway of a two-story ranch house with a porch across the front and hanging flowerpots and rocking chairs. Behind the house was a big, old-fashioned barn.

Brett parked his SUV by the back door and they entered through the kitchen where her suitcases were loudly and unceremoniously dropped to the floor.

A huge hairy beast barreled into the room, growling and snarling. His thick fur looked like it had been patched together like a quilt with several colors. Its snout wrinkled back to show off deadly fangs. Its ears were pulled back, causing its eyes to look monstrous. This was it. This was how it would end. She was destined to be dog food.

"Bear. Friend," Brett barked back at him.

The beast suddenly sat at attention.

Now that it had become a stone statue, Ginny realized it was in fact a dog, mixed breed, definitely with some mastiff blood, maybe some shepherd, and possibly a little bear. He had called it bear. It looked like a bear.

"Your room is down the hall, the first door on the right. The bathroom is across from it." Brett checked his watch. "I've got three hours to try to catch some sleep."

Ginny checked her own watch. "It's only two o'clock in the morning."

"I know. I'll be cutting it close."

After Brett closed himself behind the door at the end of the hall, Ginny pulled her suitcases into the room he'd indicated for her. She dug through them to find lightweight night clothes and her overnight bag.

Ginny tiptoed across the hall to the bathroom. She stepped under the water in the glass enclosed shower and watched the grime run off her body in ribbons. Her muscles began to relax. She hadn't realized how tense she'd become. The thought of sharing his room had tied her stomach in a knot. Thank heaven he'd shown at least a little consideration.

The room he'd assigned her was much nicer than she'd expected. It was designed to have a calming effect on its guests. The walls were painted a cool shade of green, which matched the two throw rugs on the hardwood floor. The comforter and curtains were made of the same green, gold and cream plaid fabric. There was a dresser, nightstand, and headboard in matching cherry wood. The only art in the room was a set of nature prints of a swamp. She was surprised by how beautiful a swamp could be, but then again, she wasn't stranded in a ditch in this one.

Ginny was relieved to see she looked much better in the large mirror that stood over the dresser. The bruise was still bad, but the Band-Aid covered the cut. At least now, she looked clean and fresh. She wouldn't feel so ridiculous when she faced the sheriff the next time. She would be the epitome of confidence and class.

Cuddling under the covers, Ginny realized she couldn't sleep. A cup of tea would have been nice, but she couldn't make herself leave the room. There was a beast out there somewhere. What might the bear-dog do to her if his master wasn't around to call him off? It was a chance she couldn't take and he probably didn't have a tea bag in the house anyway. She tossed and turned. She wondered if she should have ever answered Brett's first e-mail.

Mr. Silverfeather,

Attached you will find my resume, personal references, and a copy of my college transcripts. As you can see, I placed high in my class.

I'm a recent graduate of Michigan University. I have no personal attachments. I would be willing to relocate, and recertify, if needed, for the right position.

Throughout my school career I have participated in sports, fundraisers, and community activities. I would be glad to take on any added responsibilities you may require.

I am a high-energy person. No job is too big.

Virginia Dearing

Yes, it might have been the most foolish thing she'd ever done.

Just as Ginny began to drift off, a loud clatter came from down the hall. It was followed by a stream of cusswords. Someone was breaking into the house. Could this night get any worse?

Ginny threw on the light robe she'd left on the end of the bed. She groped around in the dark for a weapon. She grabbed something solid from the dresser and slowly sneaked down the hall. The light was on in the kitchen. She flattened herself against the wall and peeked around the doorframe.

"You a coffee drinker?" Brett stood by the stove looking as gorgeous, and as formidable, as he had the night before.

"All the noise woke me up."

Brett raised a brow. "Yeah, well, your hair dryer was a nice surprise at three o'clock this morning too. Here's another rule. No loud noises while I'm sleeping."

"Sorry."

"So, what's with the duck?" he asked, nodding at her hand.

Ginny looked down to find she was holding a wooden decoy duck by the neck. So much for showing confidence and class. "I thought you were an intruder."

"Well, put down the duck and step away. I already have a foolproof intruder eliminator." Brett opened the back door and Bear barreled in to find his huge bowl of kibble. He didn't seem to notice Ginny at all.

Ginny carefully stepped down from the chair she'd jumped onto. How had she forgotten about Bear?

Brett set a box of breakfast cereal, two spoons, and two bowls on the table. He opened the refrigerator to lift out a gallon of milk.

Ginny was amazed how fast he could shovel down his breakfast. This was definitely a man who lived in the fast lane. Any normal human being would have needed the Heimlich maneuver.

"I'll be home around three this afternoon," Brett said. "We'll have to get over to the courthouse before it closes. You have a birth certificate handy, I hope."

"What?"

Brett shrugged. "We have to get a marriage

18

license. No sense in wasting time."

"Oh, okay, well, those things are good for thirty days, right?"

Brett rinsed out his bowl and cup and placed them in the sink. "Yeah, after a three-day waiting period."

"Good, this black eye should be history by then." Ginny smiled. "I want to be a decent looking bride."

Brett pulled on his jacket. "Forget the bruise. We're getting married on Thursday."

"What? Why? I don't even know you yet!"

"You have to be married before school starts," he reasoned. "What would the kids think if their teacher was shacked up with the sheriff?"

Ginny hadn't thought of that. School would be starting in barely more than a week. Her reputation would be ruined before she even walked through the doors. She was desperate to keep this job. Her eyes filled with tears and her bottom lip pushed out.

When Brett saw her face he frowned. "Look, I'll make a deal with you," he said quickly. "We'll get married on Thursday, for propriety's sake, but we'll keep separate bedrooms for a month. That's a solemn promise. Would thirty days give you enough time to get to know me? Then if you still don't like me, well, the guest room would still be yours."

Ginny sniffed, which she hated to do in front of anyone. "You certainly know how to get to the point."

"Yeah, well, I don't have a lot of time to waste. I'd better get to work. See you at three." Brett grabbed his keys and rushed out the back door.

Ginny watched his hasty retreat. Had he just implied that she was a waste of his time? Besides giving her a bowl of corn flakes and a cup of coffee, Brett Silverfeather hadn't shown her an ounce of consideration. As far as Ginny was concerned, she'd be staying in the guest room for the next year.

Now here she was, left alone...in a strange

house...out in the country...without a car...under the watchful eyes of Bear.

Ginny wandered slowly around the house exploring Brett's space. You could tell a lot about a man by the way he lived. Bear followed her just as slowly. He was like having a big hairy shadow.

Looking around, she decided the man definitely had good taste. Every room was clean and well organized. The furniture was contemporary in style. The decorations were mostly Native American. With a name like Silverfeather, why hadn't she realized he might be Native American?

She investigated the kitchen, dining room, and what designers on TV call the great room. They were all decorated in browns and greens, terracotta, and flagstone. There was only one room she hadn't seen in the downstairs section of the house. It was the room at the end of the hall where Brett had disappeared the night before. Did she dare take a peek? Yes!

Holy smoke! They were the only words to enter her mind when she opened the door.

The master bedroom was built at the back corner of the house. It had the same hardwood floor as the rest of the place but these walls were painted a rich gold color. One of the outside walls was covered with a stone fireplace with bookshelves built in at each side. Ginny perused the books. He seemed to like the classics. This was the first thing she'd discovered they had in common. There were also books on criminal psychology, criminal law, and criminals in general. The man took his job seriously. Besides books, the shelves held a few plants and framed photographs. They displayed a variety of people in different places and at different times, but they appeared to be his family. The resemblance was striking.

The adjoining outside wall featured a huge

window that looked out over the woods. Matching black leather chairs sat at each side of an antique conversation table in front of the window. It was the perfect place for two people to read, eat, or just spend time together.

On the same wall as the hallway door was another door that led to a bathroom. Inside was a matching pair of sinks, a party sized Jacuzzi tub, and a shower room with water heads at two levels at each side. The room was decorated in black, gold, and glass.

On the forth wall of the bedroom stood the most fabulous bed she'd ever seen. It was huge with a thick black comforter, and several pillows in jewel colors. The headboard was reminiscent of a black iron gate with the letter S in its center. Behind the headboard, and part of the way down each side of the bed, were a variety of tall potted plants and small trees. The room actually blended with the woods outside the window.

Ginny could picture Brett sprawled in the center of that bed in all his beautiful, bronzed glory. Oh my! She needed to move on before she melted into the floorboards.

Doors at each side of the bed led to the same combination dressing room/closet. The lights had been placed to give the best advantage to full-length mirrors. Two wide columns of wooden drawers emitted a mild scent of cedar. Except for five green uniforms, a dark gray suit, three dress shirts and three pair of blue jeans, the rods were empty. One drawer in the built-in dresser held a variety of boxer shorts and black socks. A second drawer held T-shirts, half white and half various colors. The rest were empty. In the corner was a pair of old brown boots. It seemed like an awful lot of space for so little.

Next, she went up the stairs.

In the center of the upstairs area was a large space that could be used for many things, a game room, a media room, or perhaps a music room. At each end was a large bedroom and bath. All these rooms were empty. For some reason they made Ginny sad. It seemed as if the space was lonely and forgotten. No, maybe it was just waiting to be filled.

After unpacking her suitcases, Ginny was exhausted. She hadn't had a good night's sleep for the last three nights. She snuck back into Brett's room and picked up his copy of Treasure Island. Maybe she'd feel better if she relaxed for a little while.

****

The day-shift dispatcher, Coral Marshall, was on the phone when Brett passed her desk. She handed him a message.

Bernie had called to let Brett know that Ginny's car was repaired and ready to be picked up. Bernie left a lot to be desired as a human being, but he was a miracle worker when it came to cars. It would be a nice surprise for Ginny to get her car back so soon. Heaven knew she deserved some good news after the horrendous journey she'd made in the last couple of days. Her display of emotion, this morning, had probably been an after-effect of her long and disastrous trip. At least, Brett hoped so. He wasn't good with tears. It had been damned awkward.

Brett remembered how awkward it had been to write the second e-mail to Ginny. He supposed he'd handled it as well as any average man could.

Ms. Dearing,

I am interested in forwarding your information to our school board. You seem intelligent, responsible, and well qualified. I've been informed that recertification will be an easy process that can be handled once you begin.

I would be glad to tell you more about our town, and myself, after you've agreed to the added responsibilities I referred to before.

I'm sure there is a more delicate way to approach this subject, but I'm not a delicate man, and so I'll just come out with it. I need a wife.

If you would consent to marry me, I can guarantee you one year to prove yourself as an effective teacher. If all goes well, at the end of the school year you'll be offered a contract to continue.

You would have the same amount of time to decide if our marriage should also continue. If you decide to terminate the marriage after the allotted time, I guarantee it would not affect your relationship with the school or community. Also, I would be willing to incur any legal expenses necessary.

Please consider this proposal seriously.

Brett Silverfeather

Maybe he hadn't handled it as well as he'd thought. The e-mail she'd shot back nearly set his computer on fire.

Mr. Silverfeather,

I'm not sure if you are insane or simply a despicable person.

I have worked very hard to acquire my qualifications as an educator. To have you belittle those efforts by suggesting that I sell myself into human bondage is astounding. I can't believe such an arrangement would be legally binding.

What would you ask next, Mr. Silverfeather, that I send nude pictures of myself? That's not going to happen.

I picture you as a dirty old man, a sick pervert who preys on vulnerable women, or a convict getting his jollies from your jail cell.

I happen to be a young, attractive, healthy woman with more confidence and self esteem than to fall for such a ridiculous ruse.

Virginia Dearing

That's when Brett had known that Ginny had backbone. Theirs might not be a love match, if such a thing really existed, but it would be interesting. It might even be amusing, once she learned to follow a few rules. After all, weren't schoolteachers supposed to be all about rules? His certainly had.

However, thinking about those e-mails now, Brett realized he should have explained more clearly why he needed a wife. Maybe she would have understood easier and agreed a little sooner.

It had been a coincidence that Brett was helping his Aunt Marsha with her computer on the same evening she'd started looking for a new teacher. Marsha Silverfeather was the school board superintendent. The high school English teacher had just informed her that she was retiring immediately. After he'd fixed the computer problem and it was back on-line, Brett watched as Marsha perused the want ads.

"I can't believe old Ms. Carmichael retired with such short notice," Brett commented as he sipped his coffee. It was cold and he shuddered in disgust.

Marsha dropped her own foam cup into the trash. "I guess, when you get to be her age, you don't pass up an opportunity for love. Especially if that love comes with a condo on Miami Beach."

Brett squinted at the screen. "It seems like there's millions of people to choose from. What are we looking for, specifically?"

Marsha had slowly scrolled down the page. "We

need someone who's willing to move to this area immediately, and work for bottom dollar. In other words, I need someone who's well qualified and extremely desperate."

The office door had flown open without a preliminary knock. The mayor, Tom Brewster, stood filling the doorway with a red-faced scowl. He looked directly at Brett. "Where have you been?"

"Well, let's see." Brett had looked at the ceiling as he'd leaned back in his brown leather chair. "Mr. Crammer ran his truck into the maple tree in front of the Baptist church. Mrs. Simmons had a snake behind her water heater. Horace Newman stole his granddad's car and got it stuck out by the creek. I caught little Brenda Keller running sixty in a thirty-five mile an hour zone. Then, I ate lunch at Betty's. You want to hear about my afternoon?"

Tom Brewster's blood pressure appeared to be rising. "All I know is that you weren't at the city council meeting and you should've been."

Brett lowered his head and shook it slowly. "You know how much I hate those things. You cover the same old complaints every time. I'm too busy for all that nonsense. If something new comes up, I know I'll hear about it."

"Well, get ready to hear an earful, Sheriff, 'cause you were the hottest topic of the night."

Brett sat up in his chair and leaned forward. "What are you talking about?"

"Orville Dagget announced that he's running against you in the upcoming election," Brewster informed him. "He's claiming you're too young and wild. You've got no ties to the community."

"That's bull and you know it, Tom," Brett shouted as he'd jumped out of his chair, almost knocking it over. "I've lived in Three Trees all my life. My whole family lives here. Our band is based right outside the city limits, has been for over a hundred years."

"Still," Brewster shrugged, "there was the time you left for college. Now, you've been back for ten years and you still haven't started a family."

Every molecule in Brett's body turned to stone; he narrowed his eyes. "That was a low blow, Tom. You know it's not my fault."

Brewster put his hands up, palms out in surrender. "I know, I know, but Dagget sure had a lot of people listening. He pulled out all the family values cards, and you weren't there to rebut anything he said. It didn't look good for you."

During their exchange, Marsha had still been staring at the list on her computer, oblivious to anything but her own problem. "Look at this. There's a young, new teacher, up in Michigan, who seems desperate enough to do anything for a teaching job."

"Anything?" Brett remembered asking.

Now, here he was, getting ready to pick up the new schoolteacher in order to apply for a marriage license. He'd even come to work two hours early to be sure he'd be at the courthouse on time. Anybody watching would think this was something he wanted to do.

Chapter Three

"What the...? You aren't even dressed yet!"

Ginny scrambled into a ball at the end of the sofa. The dream she'd been having about Brett made her cheeks redden with embarrassment, as if he could see inside her brain. She instantly jumped to defend herself.

"Stop yelling at me, you butt-head. I fell asleep. It's the first real sleep I've had in ages."

Brett's eyes widened. "Well, isn't that nice. Here I thought schoolteachers were responsible and well-mannered. You'd better clean up your language before you meet my mother."

Ginny jumped to her feet. "Your mother is coming here...now?"

"No, but I wanted to get you up and moving." Brett looked at his watch. "You've got fifteen minutes to get ready. New rule—be ready on time when you go anywhere with me. I hate waiting."

"You've sure got a lot of rules, Mr. Bossy," she grumbled.

When Ginny re-entered the living room in a yellow peasant dress and high-heeled sandals she looked more presentable...except for the little curling iron burn under her right ear and the red spot on the side of her nose where she'd stabbed herself with the mascara wand.

Brett retrieved a tube of ointment from his bathroom and handed it to her. "For heaven's sake, you're going to look like a train wreck by the end of the week."

"I heal fast," Ginny said lamely.

After getting into the big SUV, she asked, "Can I turn on the lights and siren?"

"No."

Ginny wondered if Brett was half as nervous as she was. After all, this was a huge step they were taking. How could he be so certain they were doing the right thing? She certainly wasn't. It wasn't as though she really believed in the happily-ever-after thing. She'd seen too much as a kid to fall for all that drivel. She had hoped to someday find someone to share her life with, but she'd always pictured someone more like herself. She'd imagined a man who was quiet, studious, and professional, but not in a profession which required carrying a gun. Did he ever take the horrid thing off?

She looked over at him and wondered what his thoughts were. She wouldn't dare ask and show her insecurity. He probably didn't have an insecure bone in his body. He always looked so in control. To her embarrassment, her stomach rumbled loudly.

"No lunch?" Brett asked.

"No."

"That's all right, this shouldn't take long. After we pick up your car, we'll get back home for supper." He turned to look at her. "What did you plan for supper, by the way?"

"Supper? What did I plan?" This was something new she hadn't considered.

Brett shook his head with no further comment. He flipped his cell phone open and pressed a couple of buttons. "Hey Penny, it's the chief. I'll be by in about an hour. Can you make up a medium with pepperoni? Thanks."

"That's really not good for you, you know," Ginny mumbled.

"Neither is starving to death." Brett whispered away from the phone. To Penny he added, "Better make it a small and put a couple side salads with it."

At the courthouse, a sign on the sidewalk that read, Casper County Sheriff, pointed to the left side of the building. Ginny was curious about Brett's work place and staff, but Brett led her through the large front double doors and into the first set of offices.

A young woman sat on a stool behind the counter. She had short dark hair and a sweet smile. Over her head was a sign that read, Licenses—fishing, hunting, drivers, business and marriage. Ginny wondered if fishing might not be a better idea.

"Hey Chief...hey Ms. Dearing," the woman said, "I been wondering when you'd be by."

"Hey Connie," Brett replied. "I hear you've got another bun in the oven. With the hours you and Lucas work and the three you already have, I don't know how you find the time."

"We manage," she giggled.

Ginny realized she didn't need an introduction, which was good considering Brett hadn't offered one. However, he did say to her, "Connie here is married to Lucas Barns. I believe you met him last night."

He was the EMT who had ridden in the back of the ambulance with her.

The woman jumped in at the mention of the night before. "I'm so glad you weren't hurt real bad, Ms. Dearing. Lucas says you're just the nicest lady. Now you just gimme your birth certificate and I'll copy it while you fill out this here form. I'll have you on your way in a jiffy. I know you have a lot to do for your big day." Connie let out an ear splitting squeal. "It's just so excitin'!"

Brett didn't seem to be fazed by the squeal and ignored the comment about the big day. However, he did change the subject. "Is Ben in, Connie?"

"No, the judge stepped out for a haircut, but he told me to tell you that he'll be finished with court hearings by four o'clock on Thursday afternoon. He's put your wedding on the schedule at five." She turned to Ginny again. "This is so excitin'. Who would have thought that the chief would have picked out a pretty little Yankee girl?"

Ginny hadn't thought about their cultural differences. She suddenly became even more nervous. She'd never been called a Yankee before. Did people in Georgia hate Yankees as much as they used to?

As promised, their business was done in a jiffy, if a jiffy is about fifteen minutes long. Then they were back on the road headed to the opposite end of town from Brett's house.

The silence was killing Ginny. To entertain herself, she tried to guess what all the special gadgets were in the front of Brett's county issued SUV. It looked almost as complicated as a commercial jet cockpit.

"What made you decide to become a law enforcement officer?" she asked. "It seems like an awfully dangerous field with long hours."

It took a moment for him to answer. "I do it for the same reason as most, I guess."

"But, what is that reason?"

Brett rolled his eyes. "I decided it was best to use my powers for good instead of evil."

Okay, maybe he was also a little nervous after signing for a marriage license.

****

The big sign attached to a wooden fence read, Bernie's Engine Repair, Body Shop and Auto Salvage. What Ginny saw inside the fence looked more like a junkyard. The man waiting for them was as tall as Brett and outweighed him by about a hundred pounds. He had grizzly gray stubble on his head and face. His T-shirt was also gray, but Ginny wasn't sure that gray was its original color. His wide smile showed that he also had questionable dental hygiene.

"Touched up a few scratches and she's ready to go." He handed Brett her set of keys. "You want to take her for a test-drive to check her out, Chief?"

Brett looked at the big pink heart on her key ring with distain. "Which one is it?"

Bernie pointed at her beloved powder blue VW bug.

"You've got to be kidding." Brett turned to Ginny and gave her the keys. He also pulled a new key from his pocket. "You go on back to the house. This key will get you in. I'll pick up the pizza and be there shortly."

Ginny was disappointed that Brett seemed to hate her car. Didn't he realize it was a classic? There was nothing right about her, as far as Brett Silverfeather was concerned. She was more worried, however, about going back to his house alone.

"What if Bear attacks me when I go inside?"

"He's not going to attack you now that he knows you belong there." He gestured to her car. "Your problem will be keeping him from humping that silly looking thing."

Bernie was still laughing when Ginny drove away, her dignity a little more frayed.

****

Brett wolfed down two pieces of pizza to Ginny's one in complete silence. He looked even better in a pair of worn jeans and a faded blue T-shirt. The thin fabric did nothing to hide every well-defined muscle. When he sat back to finish his beer, Ginny decided it would be a good time to open a dialog between them.

"So, I assume you're Native American."

Brett took the last draw from his beer bottle. "You assume correctly."

"What type of Indians do you come from?"

He walked to the refrigerator for a second beer. "The red skinned, drum beating, tomahawk throwing, taking scalps kind."

"You know what I meant."

Brett sighed and studied her for a moment. "What's your ancestry?"

Ginny swallowed hard. This was one of the things she'd always wondered about herself. "I'm a mix like most people, I guess."

"Well it's a lot like that for most of us too," Brett explained. "When our land was stolen and we were forced to move west, many of our people escaped into the wilderness. Tribal lines and past disputes didn't seem to matter much anymore. It was a white against red world then. I come from the Choctaw, Cherokee, Creek and Cuban."

"Cuban? I don't think I've heard of them."

"They come from a large island, south of Florida," he said dryly.

"Oh," Ginny said, finally catching on. "You mean the Latino, Fidel Castro type of Cuban. Was there any white blood in your family?"

Brett looked at her with sober eyes. "Some of my people were known to take captives many years ago. You'll be the first in recent times."

Ginny wondered if he meant white or captive.

"Well, no pressure there," she quipped. "I thought I'd just be facing a difference in climate. But now I see our cultural differences may be an issue as well. Connie called me a Yankee. I didn't know anyone still used the term."

"Ah yes," Brett replied, "northern people never understand why southern people still hold on to the past. It seems many southerners took offense at having had their women and children raped and murdered while their men were off fighting a war. They didn't appreciate the burning of entire towns, plantations, and homesteads. They even whined a little at the theft of their valuables, livestock, and food supplies. They didn't only lose lives and property. They were also stripped of their dignity. It's a past that's hard to forget...kind of like the Trail of Tears."

"It was wartime," Ginny stated defensively. "Slaves were freed by the Union Armies."

"The slaves were freed by Lincoln, it had nothing to do with what the Union soldiers did," Brett said. "Nothing justifies the butchering of civilians. But then, what would I know? I come from a long line of savages, too."

Was he implying that her ancestors were savages? Ginny was ready to argue in defense of the north when Brett started out the back door.

"Where are you going?" she asked.

"The horses need to be brought in from the pasture and bedded down."

"You have horses?"

"They've been in the back pasture all day." Brett shook his head in the way he had a habit of doing. "You're just as observant as you are punctual, I see. I hope you do better in the classroom."

Ginny didn't get a chance to respond before the door closed behind him. He seemed to have a way of cutting her off and making everything she said and did seem ridiculous. He always came off as being in command. It reminded her of the e-mail he'd sent after she'd gotten so indignant about his proposal.

Ms. Dearing,

I can see I've offended you. Please believe that was not my intention. You have offended me in return. Let's call it a draw.

I don't know quite how to handle such a delicate proposition.

Let me begin by telling you that I'm a 32-year-old man with average looks and in good health mentally as well as physically.

I earned my degree from the University of Georgia.

I have never indulged in perverted activity or been in trouble with the law in any way. As a matter of fact, I work in law enforcement.

Attached you will find a few newspaper articles which will attest to my integrity and standing in the community.

I also take my career very seriously, Ms. Dearing. In order to continue in my position, I need to prove to a small town that I hold the family values they expect.

Three Trees, Georgia, is a nice, close-knit community which I've loved my whole life. I would never compromise the education of its youth by making this offer to just anyone. Your resume and references are impressive. I feel you'd be an asset to our school and community.

Please reconsider my offer. Time is of the essence.

Brett Silverfeather

P.S. No photos necessary.

The three attachments to the e-mail were from a newspaper called the Three Trees Gazette.

The first had been about Brett Silverfeather, lifetime resident and graduate of Three Trees High School, graduating at the top of his class at the University of Georgia with a degree in criminology.

The second had been an article that described three armed men running a meth lab who were discovered and apprehended, single handedly, by Deputy Brett Silverfeather.

The third told of the rescue of a three-year-old boy from a rapid and flooding river. Sheriff Brett Silverfeather had put his own life at risk to save the drowning child.

The man seemed to be a paragon of virtue, but Ginny still hadn't been convinced. It didn't make sense that a man like him would look for a wife on the internet. There had to be more to the story.

She tried to put the offer out of her mind for a week. During that week, several things had happened to bring Sheriff Silverfeather's offer back to the forefront.

One day after work, she'd come home to find a notice attached to her door. It had stated that the rent on Ginny's small efficiency was being raised by thirty dollars per week. The repairs needed to bring the room up to code were more costly than expected. In truth, the place should have been condemned. Another truth was, she could no longer afford it.

Two days later, she'd been informed she was being laid-off from her job at the end of the summer. The terrible economy had finally taken its toll on the small convenience store and it would be closing its doors after Labor Day. It had been the third job she'd had in the past year. She hadn't worked at one place long enough to qualify for unemployment benefits.

Three days after that, Ginny received an employment package in the mail from School Board Superintendent, Marsha Silverfeather, of Three Trees, Georgia. The salary they'd offered hadn't been as high as she would've liked and the benefits were minimal, but it offered the job she'd dreamed of for years. She'd be teaching High School English Literature.

What was one year out of her life, especially when her life was on the fast-track to nowhere? Brett Silverfeather couldn't be any worse than a lot of the men she'd dealt with over the last ten years.

Chapter Four

It was six in the morning and Brett had been awake for more than an hour. Not being one to waste time, he'd already put the coffee on, let Bear out, turned out his two horses, and mucked their stalls. Now he was finished dressing for work, except for pulling on his boots and hat.

His usual office hours were between eight and five, barring emergencies. But today, he was willing to put in a couple extra hours. In all honesty, he hoped to avoid Ginny as much as possible.

She had showered and turned in after dinner, the night before. Brett hoped she'd finally gotten a good night of sleep. However, she'd probably wake up early too, and he'd rather be at work by the time she did.

It was too hard to try to talk with her. They had nothing in common. She was a prissy little city girl. He'd met his share of those in college. The girls like her had thought it was chic to date a Native American man. It made them feel like they had something unique and exotic to show off to their friends. But they wouldn't want to take one home to meet the folks. They might run the risk of losing their allowance that week.

Since then, he'd played it safe and gone out with girls more like his mother and sisters. He'd dated girls who understood and shared his culture; girls who could appreciate the values he lived by. At least that's what he'd thought.

Of course, it had been a long time ago. He'd only dated one woman in the last four years. She'd been the only woman with whom he'd shared his dreams. He'd looked into those deep dark eyes and been lost. Diana had claimed to want all the same things he did—home, family, and tradition. Then she'd ripped out his heart and stomped on it, all for a place in the spotlight. That had been a year ago. He hadn't had the urge to touch a woman since. At least, not until Virginia Dearing had shown up at the clinic, looking like a drowned rat. He was baffled and irritated by his attraction to her. It wasn't supposed to be like that.

When he'd come up with this idea, to marry for the benefit of his career, he'd thought it wouldn't matter who the woman was. They'd both benefit by the deal professionally and hopefully enjoy each other's company. They'd co-exist peacefully and maybe even take care of each other's physical needs. He'd chosen a woman in a particular age range who would be acceptable to the community and the job for which she was needed. He hadn't counted on a girl like Ginny. Her world was several galaxies away from his.

Maybe he should have asked her for a photograph in his e-mails after all. Beyond the bumps and bruises she'd recently received, she was as delicate as a china teacup. Her skin was so fair it was practically translucent. She didn't even have a freckle that showed. Sometimes he found himself mesmerized by the tiny blue veins that showed at her temples. They made her seem almost ethereal.

He'd never known a woman as small as her. The clothes she'd left in the laundry room were size five. His sisters had had dolls that wore larger dresses. He'd always gone for full figured girls, but now he found her compact figure intriguing. It was almost frightening to think of touching a woman that small.

He found himself staring at her hair a lot. Rather than the wealth of dark hair he was used to,

Ginny had a short blunt style the color of corn silk. He'd heard a lot of blonde jokes, and from what he'd seen from Ginny so far, he hadn't found the proof to dispel them. However, he'd also seen her college transcripts and they were outstanding. She obviously had a fully functional brain, academically. What was it that held her back in the real world? She seemed too naive and innocent to have achieved all she had.

The thing that got under his skin most was her eyes. They were the most beautiful shade of pale green he'd ever seen. Those eyes spoke to his soul. He could tell they held secrets she may have never shared. Brett wondered if he'd ever know what those secrets were. Some things were better left alone. He'd never planned to get too close to her. Not in that way, at least.

He honestly didn't know what he'd been thinking when he'd proposed this arrangement. He'd been desperate to keep his job. Perhaps he'd also been alone a little too long.

Brett started down the hall to the kitchen, still thinking about Ginny. He wondered how she'd ever survived in the real world, as fragile as she was.

Just then, Ginny burst out of her room and ran straight into him. She gave him a sleepy one-eyed glare. "Get out of my way, you big ox. I have to use the bathroom."

Okay, maybe fragile wasn't exactly the right word.

Brett had missed his chance to escape quietly. As long as he was still home, he might as well make a decent breakfast. If yesterday was any indication, she might starve to death otherwise. He cooked the meal and had it on the table by the time she emerged from the bathroom. He hoped the morning meal would serve as a peace offering.

When Ginny walked into the kitchen, she was

dressed and ready for the day.

"I didn't realize I was hungry until I smelled your cooking," she said, as she sat at the table. She picked up her fork and froze when she looked down at her plate. "What is this?"

"Breakfast," Brett said as he salted and peppered his food.

"I figured that much out myself." Ginny ran her fork through the grainy yellow puddle next to the two fried eggs on her plate. "What I mean is, what is this?"

"This," Brett stated, "is cheese grits, the main staple of a good southern breakfast. Let me guess, you don't eat cheese."

Brett cut his eggs into small pieces and mixed them into his own puddle of grits. Then he put a forkful into his mouth. He gave a long, low groan of pleasure. He didn't gag or keel over. That was a good sign.

"Cheese isn't a problem. It's the grits I'm not sure about. I've heard mention of them, but I've never actually seen them before." He shoveled another forkful into his mouth. She curled her lip in disgust. "Does everyone down here mix their food together that way?"

Brett took a swallow of coffee to wash down a bite of toast. "Look, you can eat them mixed or on the side, or you can just not eat them at all. As far as I'm concerned, you can go hungry."

"No need to get snippy," Ginny huffed.

Brett glared at her. So much for the peace offering. "Snippy? Did you say I'm being snippy? I don't recall insulting your cooking." He paused for a moment. "Oh, that's right. You haven't even made a sandwich since you've been here."

"I've never lived with anyone before. I'm not used to cooking."

Brett threw his napkin onto the table. "I know

you're skinny, but you have to have eaten occasionally. You still seem to have enough energy to annoy me at every turn."

"I'm not trying to annoy you. I intend to do my share. I can make a few things, but..." Ginny looked away, embarrassed. "I've looked everywhere and I can't find the microwave oven."

"There's a good reason for that," Brett growled. "I don't have one. When a person cooks a real meal they use a real stove. That's what I expect you to do tonight. I'll be home by six unless I have an emergency, in which case, I'll call you. But, come hell or high water, it's your turn to cook supper."

****

Despite the way her day had started, it felt good being back behind the wheel of her car. If it weren't for the teaching position she'd been promised, she would get back on the interstate and keep driving. Instead, she'd do what she did best...She'd shop.

Ginny only had two days to find a nice dress for her wedding. Luckily, none of the stores in Three Trees looked to be overpriced. She had a choice between two places along Main Street which sold clothing; the Baptist Church Secondhand Thrift Shop or Mandy's Fashion Emporium. She chose Mandy's.

A young woman, with long black hair, came around the counter. She was about the same age as Ginny, but taller by a good six inches and had a fuller figure. The most attractive thing about the woman, though, was her warm smile.

"Hi, I'm Mandy Silverfeather. What can I help you find today?"

"Hi Mandy, I'm Ginny Dearing. Are you related to Brett Silverfeather?" Ginny blushed with embarrassment. The name Silverfeather couldn't be very common.

"Isn't everyone?" Mandy laughed. "I'm a cousin.

Our fathers were brothers. You must be the new schoolteacher he's marrying. I've been hoping you'd come by. It's so nice to meet you. I didn't know what to expect. The chief has been pretty tightlipped about you. Don't take offense though. He's not one to share his business."

"Everyone seems to be a little surprised. I get the impression they weren't expecting a small, white, northern woman." Ginny couldn't make herself use the word Yankee as Connie had. The word had never really been a part of her vocabulary until yesterday. She looked around nervously. "I take it I'm not Brett's usual type."

"He hasn't had any usual type lately, and that's what surprised me the most. News of a wedding was a real shocker." Mandy patted Ginny's arm. "Don't worry, though. You'll fit in just fine. Three Trees is a nice town. I've lived here all my life and I wouldn't want to be anywhere else."

That was the thing Ginny wanted almost as much as teaching, to fit in to a nice place. Meeting Nora, and now Mandy, seemed to be a good start. She hoped all of Brett's family and friends would be as welcoming as those two had.

"Maybe you can help me," Ginny said. "I need a nice dress for the wedding. Is there something...traditional I should look for? I don't really know what's expected for an occasion like this."

"From what Connie tells me, it'll be a simple service in the judge's chambers." Mandy looked over her racks of clothing and looked Ginny up and down. She took Ginny's hand and pulled her toward the back of the store. "Something simple, but chic, would be best. I have a few lightweight suits you should look at. They're not only perfect for the occasion but also for the season."

They found Ginny's size and flipped through a

few choices, but were soon interrupted by two women who entered the store with their teenage daughters. Ginny wondered if she might see the younger girls in her classroom next week.

While she looked over the rack of suits, Mandy helped the girls pick out a few pairs of jeans, and shirts to try on.

The mothers busied themselves in the lingerie section. She noticed they were stealing glances at her and whispering. She supposed a lot of people were curious about her and wished she could hear what they were saying. She'd forgotten the old adage her mother used to use. Be careful what you wish for, you just may get it.

Wanting to impress the other ladies, Ginny picked out the most beautiful and expensive suit on the rack. It was made of soft white linen. It had a plain straight skirt, but the blazer had pale green piping around the lapels and slit pockets. She already owned shoes and a bag that would look perfect with it. With a price tag of $175.00 she couldn't really afford it, but it would have cost five times as much in the city. And after all, this was for her wedding. Now she just hoped it would fit.

When the teenage girls took a break from the dressing room, Ginny slipped inside. The two women, looking through the lingerie, didn't realize she could hear them clearly through the thin wall at their backs.

"Diana said he was the most talented man she'd ever slept with," one woman giggled, "and his equipment is spectacular."

That comment perked up Ginny's ears. Conversation among the housewives of Three Trees was more interesting than she'd expected.

"That may be so," the second woman replied dryly, "but Clint heard him tell his uncle he'd never trust another woman as long as he lived. You can't have a good marriage without trust."

Ginny felt sorry for the girl they were talking about, even if she didn't know her. She hated to think of the heartache she'd be in for. It was true; trust was the cornerstone of a relationship.

"Who needs love and trust when you've got the chief in your bed? The man is built like a Roman God. And that face... How many times have you closed your eyes and pictured him in your husband's place? Don't lie. We all do it.

"Diana was such a fool to give him up. However, this schoolteacher does seem too sweet and pretty to settle for second place, doesn't she? Poor thing..."

Ginny felt a lump in her throat. They were talking about Brett. They were talking about her. Her stomach tightened painfully. Why did it matter that Brett had been involved with someone else? She didn't even know if she liked him.

One of the women spoke again. "I wonder how it feels to sleep in another woman's bed. Diana would have been the one picking out a wedding dress right now if she'd stuck around."

Another woman's bed? Ginny realized her anxiety wasn't just because of Brett's romantic history. It was because she was a replacement bride...and everyone seemed to know it but her.

She quickly changed back into her own clothes and took the white suit to the cash register. She was still getting married because she still needed the job. It was all she had and she'd worked too hard to walk away from it. Nothing else mattered.

As the women walked further away, one of them said, "The chief and Diana were a perfect couple. It's such a shame."

Ginny wondered why their words hurt her heart, when her heart hadn't been involved in this deal to begin with.

Mandy had also overheard the two women.

Ginny could tell by the disgusted look she gave them. Maybe people all over town were saying the same things. It wouldn't be the first time she'd been the subject of gossip, but she'd been hoping things would be different here.

"Don't worry about those two," Mandy said, as Ginny fumbled through her purse without making eye contact with her. "They're just a couple of old busybodies."

Mandy raised her voice to address the two other women. "Are you ladies buying anything today or did you just come by to gossip like a couple of old geese?"

The women had the good sense to look embarrassed.

After putting her garment bag in her car, Ginny walked further down the sidewalk to get to the grocery store. Surely there was something she could find to make a decent meal and save this day from total disaster.

At the second shop she passed, an old man waved excitedly from the other side of the large window. Ginny looked around to find it was a hardware store. She didn't want to be rude, but she didn't need hardware. She waved back politely.

"Come inside," the old man said, as he opened the door. "I've been waiting all day for you to come by. I heard you'd picked your car up from Bernie's shop yesterday and I knew you'd want to explore your new town."

Ginny looked over each shoulder to make sure he was talking to her. No one else was nearby.

The man must have been in his late seventies or early eighties. He was tall, lean and dark. His skin was as brown and lined as old leather. Salt and pepper hair hung loosely down the back of his colorful Indian print shirt. Ginny found him strangely attractive for a man his age. He didn't seem threatening. As a matter of fact, he seemed quite welcoming. Ginny needed a friend at that moment and so she stepped inside.

"My name is Noah Silverfeather," the man said. "I'm Little Chief's—I mean Brett's grandfather. You can call me Poppy. Everyone in town calls me Poppy."

Ginny remembered what Nora Baxter had said. She offered him her hand. "I'm Ginny."

"A handshake is not what a grandfather needs," Poppy said gently as he circled his arms around her for a hug.

Ginny had never had a grandfather of her own. Not one she'd ever heard of anyway. The warm, affectionate embrace overwhelmed her. Before she knew what was happening, she was leaking tears onto the front of his nice shirt. What was wrong with her? She hadn't cried in years and now she was acting like a little kid with a skinned knee, in front of a total stranger.

Poppy led her to an old rocking chair in the corner and sat her down. He handed her a clean white handkerchief.

"Tell me what's bothering you, little dove."

Ginny let the floodgates open. She told Poppy everything that had happened—all the mistakes she'd made, how much Brett seemed to dislike her, all of his rules, even an edited version of the conversation in the dress shop. The old man was like a hypnotist who could pull the thoughts and emotions from her mind without her ability to resist.

"Fear is a good thing," Poppy said. "It protects us. But you are letting your fear direct your actions, and that's not good. Instead you should ignore these ignorant people until they find out who you really are. Try to think of your new life here as an adventure. Each young mind you touch will carry you further along the road to the end of your journey."

Ginny sniffled. "There's nothing I've ever wanted more, than to teach. But to have that chance, I have to marry Brett. How can I live with a man who wishes I were someone else?"

Poppy lowered his head and shook it slowly, the way Brett had a tendency to do. The gesture made Ginny's heart ache a little more.

"I shouldn't tell you this," he said, "but I don't believe Brett had true love for the other woman. He loved the future he envisioned with her. When she left him, his pride was hurt, not his heart. Now he's being stubborn to protect his pride. Pride is a powerful thing in a man, especially a Silverfeather man. Once he learns to trust you, he will see that future with you."

"But he told someone he'd never trust another woman again. What can I do to make him trust me?"

Poppy smiled gently. "Trust is a hard thing to earn, especially when you're dealing with such a stubborn man. The only way to earn his trust is through honesty, caring, and a lot of patience."

"I wish there was some way I could make him see that I want to make the effort."

They sat silently for a moment, and then Poppy smiled broadly. "You should give him a gift, a wedding gift. It should be something you would give only to him."

"I don't know him well enough to know what would suit him. I wouldn't know what to give him. Besides that, I don't have much money left."

Poppy took her hand and led her behind the counter of the store. "I know him better than anyone. I have the perfect thing for you to give him. And you can have the 90% family discount. Just don't tell the rest of the family or they'll want it too."

Ginny was much happier and more confident that evening…until Brett returned home.

She could tell right away he was in a bad mood.

The mud smeared down the front of his uniform and bloody scrapes on the heels of his hands were the tip off.

Jumping from the kitchen chair where she'd been reading, she asked, "What happened to you?"

He took the time to pour kibble into Bear's bowl before he answered. "The Harvey boys blew up Mr. Crammer's henhouse with a pipe bomb," he finally said. "It's ridiculous what kids can find on the internet these days. Anyway, we had to chase them down in the bog and I tripped over a tree root."

"Was anyone hurt?" She pointed at his bloody hands. "I mean, besides you."

"I only got a couple little scrapes. Mr. Crammer lost over a dozen laying hens. That's how the old man makes his living. Kids don't have any respect anymore. I have half a mind to send those boys to juvenile detention this time."

Thinking like the schoolteacher Ginny wanted to be, she instantly defended the boys. "Those places are just training grounds for mixed-up kids to learn to become true criminals. Being locked away isn't going to do those boys or Mr. Crammer any good. What they need is patience, understanding and a little guidance. Why don't you make them rebuild the henhouse and work to replace the hens? I firmly believe the punishment should fit the crime."

Brett's answer burst out louder than he'd intended. "I'm not in the business of coddling the next generation of terrorists, and I don't need you to tell me how to do my job. Let's make that a new rule. I won't tell you how to teach and you won't tell me how to enforce the law."

Ginny backed away with a cringe. "Sorry."

Brett didn't like the look of fear in Ginny's eyes. He lowered his voice. "It's been a long day. I'm tired and dirty. I'm going to take a shower."

Ginny was glad she'd made a nice big dinner for

Brett. Men always felt better after a big meal. While he showered and changed, she set the table. She lit a candle in the new centerpiece she'd picked up for a dollar at the Baptist Secondhand Thrift Shop and opened a bottle of chilled white wine.

Brett seemed more relaxed when he returned. He sniffed the air and then he looked around the kitchen suspiciously. "Does something smell strange in here to you?"

"Nope, just my new candle and dinner," Ginny grinned.

Brett lifted the lid off a skillet on the stove. "What is this stuff?"

"Gravy. There's chicken in the oven too. I've been cooking all afternoon."

Brett lifted the skillet and tilted it sideways. The sludge stuck to the bottom. "Gravy isn't supposed to cook all afternoon."

He set the skillet on the floor beside Bear's bowl. The dog sniffed it and backed away.

"If Bear won't eat it, neither will I."

Then he opened the oven door and slid out the roasting pan. "Chicken jerky might be good, though." He lifted another lid from a pot on the stove and used a large spoon to play with the loose, lumpy concoction. "Don't tell me...boiled potatoes."

Ginny groaned. "I didn't think it would be so hard. Nothing turned out the way I'd expected it to."

Brett took a few slices of bacon and an onion out of the refrigerator. He chopped them both up and threw them into a fresh skillet. Then he grated a carrot over the top.

"What are you doing?" Ginny asked.

Brett poured a large dose of the wine into the pot of potatoes before answering. "Your potatoes are almost soup. I'm helping them along."

He drained the skillet mixture and dumped it into the pot as well. Then he cleaned his skillet and

48

proceeded to grill cheese sandwiches. The easy way he moved around the kitchen made her feel inadequate and useless.

Ginny had once had a teacher who'd said she was book smart, but lacked common sense, and it was true. She'd seen ten-year-olds with better culinary skills than she had. It embarrassed her, to say the least. Brett was probably rethinking his decision to marry her at this very moment.

"You make it look so easy," Ginny said.

"Our family spends most of their time in the kitchen. I guess I just picked it up." Brett's voice softened as he thought back to his childhood. "Didn't you ever watch your mom cook?"

When Ginny found herself in an awkward situation she often made a joke of the truth. "Well, if you wanted hot dogs and boxed macaroni and cheese, you should have said so. She could also do canned soup and fish stick sandwiches."

Brett looked at her with a serious expression. "So that's what stunted your growth."

Chapter Five

Brett could hear the shower running in the guest bathroom as he made his morning coffee. He didn't have a lot of time and decided to put out cereal for breakfast. Meals had become a major issue in his house. It suddenly seemed awfully ridiculous to him. He'd been taking care of himself for more than fifteen years.

He'd made most of the meals for his roommates when he'd gone away to college. Puttering in the kitchen had made him feel more at home in the old house he and five other students shared. Now, one small woman enters the scene and he's turned into a caveman.

He'd never been the kind of guy who thought a woman should be chained to the stove. But, he'd also never imagined a woman would grow up without the basic skills his sisters had picked up naturally. His sisters, Julie and Nina, had helped in the kitchen as soon as they could climb onto a chair beside their mother. Could what Ginny said last night, about hot dogs and fish sticks, be true? What kind of mother would do that to a kid? If she'd been joking, he didn't find it the least bit amusing. To his mind, that kind of diet constituted child neglect, maybe even abuse. No man in the world would put up with that. Didn't she have a father?

It suddenly occurred to Brett that he knew absolutely nothing about Ginny aside from her resume. What kind of family did she come from? He'd always thought all Midwestern families were the conventional white-bread types; middle class,

Republican, suburban kind of people. Maybe it had been narrow-minded of him. They would have to have a long talk and that was one thing he wasn't very good at. Brett was a dynamo in the interrogation room, but one on one sharing of personal information was beyond his comfort zone. He would have to make the effort if he was going to be married to the woman. It would have to wait until he had more time, though.

He had a lot of work to catch up on and plans to make at the office. With so little manpower it was hard to take time off. Everyone in the department was shocked when he'd announced he'd be taking the evening off after the wedding and through the next day. That still wasn't much time for the two of them to get to know each other, but he owed her at least that much just for agreeing to this arrangement. And it wasn't as if they were taking a proper honeymoon anyway...dammit. He was already regretting his promise of a month in separate bedrooms.

There he was, being a caveman again.

Ginny entered the kitchen with damp hair and the scent of lavender soap. She was surprised to find a bowl already filled with cereal at her place. Milk and sugar sat in the middle of the breakfast table along with ripe bananas. Brett looked as handsome as always, pouring coffee into her cup.

His long braid hung over his shoulder as he leaned his head down. She'd never been particularly attracted to men with long hair, but with Brett she couldn't help wondering what his hair would be like, loose from its binding and brushing over her skin. She'd never known a man with waist length hair. Everything about him seemed as wild as the animals that prowled the nearby woods. She imagined he would be just as wild while making love and it thrilled her a little, but scared her a lot. She'd known dominant men before and they weren't kind, considerate, or gentle. She was beginning to wonder if any man was really like the ones in the paperback novels she sometimes read late at night. If any man could be, though, she wished it would be him. He was so beautiful and soon he'd be her husband.

Ginny jumped when Brett suddenly spoke.

"Are you all right?"

"Yes, of course. Why do you ask?" Ginny was embarrassed by her breathless voice.

"I don't know, you looked a little pale and spaced out there for a minute. Did you sleep well?"

Ginny gave him her most charming smile. "That must be it. I slept so well, I'm not fully awake yet."

Brett gave her a suspicious scowl, and then moved on to what was on his mind. "I was thinking it might be nice to go out for dinner tonight. There's a nice steak house, south of town."

Ginny's eyes grew as round as saucers. "Dinner out. Me and you...like a date?"

Her voice had reached a higher octave with each word. That would have usually annoyed Brett, but instead he felt guilty. Her excitement punctuated how badly he'd neglected her. He realized he hadn't done a single thing to make her happy to be here in Three Trees. He hadn't even tried to make her feel welcome, and yet, he expected her to be his wife. He knew he'd never be able to love her, but he could at least make their coexistence pleasant. Hell, if he played his cards right through the rest of the month, she might be willing to peel off those sexy silk boxers and the tight little tank top she was currently wearing.

His inner caveman had reared his ugly head again.

Brett shook his head to put it back on track. "I should be able to leave work at about five o'clock today." Brett pulled his hat low over his eyes. He opened the back door to leave, but turned to add. "I'd like to show you off a little. Why don't you drive in and meet my day shift before they leave. We can leave your car there and pick it up on our way home."

Ginny was speechless. Brett wanted to take her out and show her off. She had to look spectacular and make him proud. She couldn't screw up this chance to bond with him as a friend. He might not have any other interest in her, but they could at least enjoy each other's company. Maybe, with enough playacting, they could even put some of the gossip in town to rest. She'd show those old biddies she wasn't just a pathetic replacement.

After finishing the book she'd started, Ginny looked at the clock. It was only ten o'clock. How was she going to fill her day before her dinner with Brett? She decided that if she couldn't impress him with a decent meal, she could at least show him that she was a top-notch housekeeper.

She started in the kitchen, scrubbing every surface and mopping the floor. Soon she'd dusted, swept and mopped her way through the dining room and great room. After her bedroom was finished she moved on to the bathroom. Rolling up the used towels, she wondered if she should continue on to Brett's private domain. Before she could decide, she was interrupted by a series of barks and scratching at the back door.

Bear stood happily on the back porch covered in mud from his belly to the ground. At his feet was the carcass of a dead squirrel. He nudged the unfortunate furry creature closer to Ginny's feet with his nose and then pranced into her freshly cleaned kitchen, mud and all.

Ginny hadn't ever owned a dog and wasn't sure what to do with the gruesome gift. She decided to leave it where it was, for Brett to pick up, and use the front door for the rest of the day.

The muddy tracks across her clean floor led her through every room she'd just cleaned until she got to the bathroom. There was Bear, standing like a hairy statue in her tub. He seemed to be wearing a quiet crestfallen look, as though he knew a bath was a necessary evil. Not knowing what else to do, Ginny grabbed her bottle of lavender scented body wash and got to work. It was one o'clock by the time she'd gotten the dog, and the house, back in order.

Ginny was finally able to prepare herself for her dinner date with Brett. Bear insisted on not just watching, but participating in the process. To Ginny, he looked as good as she did with his fur blown dry to a fluff and bright red nail polish on all four paws. He was particularly proud of the red calico bandanna tied around his neck. She could tell by the way he panted happily as he licked her bare toes. He even smelled good, which Ginny considered the most outstanding improvement.

At three o'clock, to her annoyance there was a knock on the back door. The back door meant a personal visit. She couldn't imagine who it could be.

Ginny opened the door to find three women standing on the porch studying the dead squirrel. Two of the women were in their twenties and one was middle-aged, but just as beautiful. They all had black hair and skin the same color as Brett's. They wore long colorful skirts and sleeveless blouses. Ginny felt out of place in her tan linen slacks and red silk camisole style top. She was embarrassed to realize she was still barefoot.

"It looks like Bear's been out hunting," the youngest woman said, indicating the deceased squirrel. "You must really rate. All I've ever gotten from him was the back half of a barn mouse."

"I'm sure she'd love to hear all about it," the second young woman said, as she walked past Ginny into the kitchen. "Personally, I'd rather sit in the air-conditioning and have a cup of tea."

The older woman rolled her eyes. "Forgive my daughters' bad manners. I did try to bring them up better, but they tend to make themselves at home in their brother's house."

Their brother's house? These two young women were Brett's sisters! That meant the other woman was his mother...Ohmigod! Ginny's heart leaped into panic mode. She didn't know what to say, what to do, how to act.

"I'm Julie Mantooth," the older of the two sisters said, as she filled the teakettle. She looked the most like Brett with her waist length braid and statuesque build. "I'm third in line. The brat rummaging through the pantry is the baby of the family, Nina Whitetail. We decided to come over and check you out."

"Julie!" her mother scolded, "don't make Brett's bride feel uncomfortable." She turned to Ginny with the same amber eyes as Brett's, but she was shorter than her daughters and her features were more rounded and soft. "My name is Emma Silverfeather. I'm Brett's mother, and these two are my unruly daughters. We just wanted to welcome you and make sure you have everything you need for tomorrow. My son insists on a private ceremony, but I don't want you to think we don't support the two of you...although I do find the whole situation quite strange."

"I found them!" Nina emerged from the pantry with a bag of pecan shortbread cookies. She knew exactly where to find a plate to put them on.

Ginny wished she were as familiar with this kitchen as this bubbly girl with hair that floated around her shoulders like a sheet of silk. Ginny felt awkward and out of place. They seemed more at home in the house then she did.

"So, tomorrow is the big event," Nina continued, "Are you nervous? I can just imagine the river of tears that will flow down Main Street when it's over. Every single woman in town has had their eye on the chief. Nobody ever thought they had a chance with him after he hooked up with Diana, though."

"Nina!" Mrs. Silverfeather chided. "Stuff a cookie in it."

"Sorry."

They all sat around the table with the cookies and tea. The two sisters entertained Ginny with stories about the family, especially Poppy.

Poppy had been a wild one, back in his younger days. He finally settled down twenty years ago when he took in Brett's family. Brett's father had been a forest ranger and Poppy's oldest of two sons and three daughters. He'd been killed by an escaped convict hiding from the police in the woods. The three Silverfeather women agreed that was the incident that had prompted Brett's interest in law enforcement.

Ginny also found out the judge who was to marry them the next day, was Brett's uncle, Ben Silverfeather. He was Poppy's only surviving son.

The school superintendant who had offered her the job, Marsha Silverfeather, was Ben's wife. They had two children, Mandy, from the fashion emporium and a son who was away at college.

Poppy's three daughters had all married and were scattered in other towns around South Georgia with their families.

Brett and his siblings had all decided to stay in Three Trees, where they'd been born and raised.

Nina and Julie beamed with pride when they talked about their brothers. Jake was two years younger than Brett. He ran the local newspaper with his wife. They had three young children.

Julie ran her own day care center from her

home. She was married to a lawyer and had two small sons who were currently with their other grandparents until the weekend.

Nina was the assistant manager at the grocery store in town. She was married to a construction manager. They'd only been married for eighteen months and were expecting their first child in six months.

Ginny knew she wouldn't be able to remember all the names and information she'd been given. The only name swimming through her mind was Diana. The woman Brett—to use Nina's words—had hooked up with. The woman whose bed she was sleeping in, according to the two customers at Mandy's store. From everyone's reaction to her coloring and background, Ginny had to assume that Diana was a Native American like these women. She had probably fit in much better than Ginny ever would.

Across the table, Mrs. Silverfeather was absentmindedly stirring her cooling tea and staring into space. She wore a pensive look and hadn't spoken since they'd all sat down. Ginny wondered if her future mother-in-law was disappointed her eldest son chose to marry outside of his race.

"Mrs. Silverfeather, I know I'm not the kind of woman you would have chosen for Brett. I'm not very domestic and I don't know anything about your culture. But, I am going to try to learn and make this experience as pleasant as I can for both of us."

Mrs. Silverfeather patted Ginny's hand. "I appreciate your effort, dear. I understand it's hard to get a start these days, especially when you've come to a place so unlike what you're used to. You seem like a nice girl. I know you'll try, but I also know my stubborn son won't make it easy for you. He's determined to close his heart off from any possible happiness. I had hoped all my children would be married and bonded before I died, but I guess three out of four is the best I can hope for."

"Oh, Mom," Nina groaned. "You'll probably outlive all of us. Besides that, Brett could possibly pull his head out of his butt and have a change of heart."

"Nina!" Mrs. Silverfeather looked at Ginny with a devastated expression and then turned to her daughter. "Do you want Ginny to think we're a bunch of-of...?"

"Savages?" Nina supplied for her tongue-tied mother. "Pigheaded men aren't exclusive to the state of Georgia, Mom. And chances are pretty good that Ginny's heard worse things. Schoolteachers have evolved over the years, you know."

"She's right, Mom," Julie added with a grin. "She might as well know from the get-go that we aren't perfect. Living with the chief, she'll learn to use some colorful language of her own. If she doesn't know it already, she can learn from the best."

Ginny didn't comment about the language. She had a different subject on her mind. "What did you mean when you mentioned bonding, Mrs. Silverfeather?"

Mrs. Silverfeather was glad for the change in subject. "We marry by the white man's law, and if it's a true love, we bond in the way of our own people."

"Bonding is more important to us than the marriage vows," Nina said.

"That's right," Julie interjected, "the promises a couple make to each other when they bond is witnessed by the whole band, or family. A bond can never be broken and can only happen once in a person's life."

"If you break the bond," Nina added, "you might as well move to China. The whole band would turn against you. We take it very seriously. It's better not to bond at all than to do it halfheartedly."

Mrs. Silverfeather nodded. "That's why I always say to be very careful what promises you make. It's a huge commitment and should be thought through carefully."

Ginny glanced down at her watch. It was 4:45. "Oh damn! I'm going to be late again! Brett will have my head this time!"

All three women facing Ginny around the table burst out laughing.

Mrs. Silverfeather stood to leave. She surprised Ginny with a warm hug. "It looks like our work here is done, ladies. We've corrupted Brett's woman enough for one day."

****

At five-thirty, Brett checked his watch again. He should have expected Ginny to screw up. It seemed to be what she did best. He wondered, not for the first time, if he'd made a mistake by suggesting her for the teaching position. She was highly qualified, but her personal habits sucked.

The phone on his desk rang. Brett figured it was finally Ginny with another lame excuse for being late. Seconds later he wished it had been.

"Sheriff, this is Officer Bryant from the Georgia Highway Patrol. We have a lady in our custody by the name of Virginia Dearing. She says she knows you, and we were wondering if we could drive her over to your office. It's a lot closer than our office, and we just started our shift. We kind of hate to go all the way back."

Brett leaned back in his chair and squeezed his eyes shut. He felt a sudden headache coming on. "What are the charges, Officer Bryant?"

"Well sir, it started with speeding. She might have gotten off with a warning, but then she opened her purse and it turned into a concealed weapons charge. I'd just as soon avoid the paperwork if you'd be willing to handle this at your end."

Brett swallowed two aspirins with a cold cup of coffee and shuddered.

"Well hell," he groused. "Why not?"

Fifteen minutes later, Ginny was marched through the outer office with her hands cuffed behind her back. She wouldn't look Brett in the eye. Brett showed her and Officer Bryant to his office.

At the door, Officer Bryant hesitated. "I really need to get back on the road. If you can handle things from here, I'll just take my cuffs back."

When he started to take the keys from his pocket, Brett put his hand on the officer's arm. "Wait a minute," he said. Brett took a matching set of cuffs out of a leather pouch on his belt. "Just take mine. I think I'd like to leave those on her for a few more minutes."

As soon as Officer Bryant closed the door behind him, Brett nudged Ginny back into a chair. She started to mutter an apology, but Brett cut her off. "You may not care about my reputation and the fact that I'm coming up for re-election. You may not care that I've been humiliated in front of the people who work under me. You may not care that news of this incident is already traveling all over town. But have you given the least little thought to the fact that you're ruining your own reputation in the only town that has offered you a teaching position?"

Ginny burst into tears. Between sniffles she tried to explain. "I was in a hurry because I didn't want to be late..."

Brett was determined not to let her tears sway him. "You've got a bad habit of being late," he yelled, "I told you being on time was a rule. So why didn't you give yourself enough time?"

Still sniffling, Ginny yelled back. "I couldn't just throw your mom and sisters out of the house. I didn't even know they were coming."

Brett lowered his head and shook it. He could

just imagine the women in his family steamrolling their way into his house to meet the new woman in his life. She couldn't have gotten them out with dynamite. But, that still didn't explain the weapons charge.

When he looked up, tears were streaming down her pink cheeks. Brett's gaze followed one of those tears all the way down to the corner of her mouth. He'd noticed her lips before, but now, because she was crying, they were a little swollen and red. They looked so incredibly soft. He wondered if her lips would be like that after a thorough kiss or when she was sexually aroused. He wondered how they would feel against his. He had the mad urge to find out, right here, right now, but he struggled to curb the urge.

On a hiccup Ginny whispered, "I'm sorry."

Brett took a tissue from the box on his desk. He held it to her nose. "Blow."

A tap sounded on the door behind him. When he opened it, Officer Bryant was back on the other side. "I guess I was in too much of a rush and forgot to give you this." Bryant handed him the weapon she'd been caught with, nodded a quick good-bye, and walked away.

The knife had a solid bone handle and a wide blade about eight inches long. It had a soft leather sheath with laces to fasten it onto a belt and around a leg. The beading was a mix of black, gold and green in the shape of an eagle. Most people would think it was a hunting knife, but Brett knew Indian warriors wore knives like this when they rode out with a war party. It was an amazing piece of craftsmanship; a piece of American history; a piece of art.

"What are you doing with this?" he asked Ginny.

"It was supposed to be a surprise. It's your wedding gift. For...after our wedding tomorrow."

Chapter Six

On the outside Brett looked as cool as a spring breeze, but on the inside he was fighting the urge to pace the floor and bite his fingernails. He glanced at the large clock hanging on the wall of his uncle's chamber. Ginny had ten minutes. Would she arrive on time this time?

Ginny certainly came with challenges, but within the next hour, she'd be his wife. He wondered for the thousandth time if he was doing the right thing. He still didn't know anything about her except she seemed to be having a hard time adjusting. He had the feeling it was mostly his fault. He was used to dealing with lawbreakers and had a tendency to be hard at times. The fact that he felt forced into marriage made him harder on Ginny than he had any cause to be. He didn't know why she'd put up with him, except she was desperate for the teaching job. Didn't she realize she could have gotten the job on her own merit?

Everyone she'd met so far seemed to like her. People constantly stopped him on the street to say so. His mother had even called that morning to tell him what a nice time she and his sisters had had talking with Ginny. She had also explained they were to blame for Ginny being behind schedule the day before.

His very own dog even preferred to spend his time with Ginny these days. Bear had slept outside her bedroom door all night with his fluffy coat, bandanna collar and red nail polish. He would have to talk to her about the nail polish—that and the fact that his dog smelled girly.

Who was he kidding? He didn't know how to talk to her.

His only long-term relationship had been with Diana, and she'd done most of the talking. The only things required of him were the things he could take care of between the sheets.

He shook off that train of thought. Now was not a good time to think about Diana. It was definitely a bad time to think about sex. He had a marriage to get started today, and still had a lot of the thirty days of abstinence left to endure before he could even approach his new wife. Even when his time was up, he wasn't sure Ginny would want to have anything to do with him.

As soon as he'd removed the handcuffs yesterday, Ginny had gone straight home. She hadn't come out for dinner last night, or breakfast this morning. He'd left a note saying he would send a deputy to pick her up so she wouldn't have to bring her car into town, but for all he knew, she could be halfway back to Michigan. He couldn't say he'd blame her. He'd acted like an ass so far, but after thinking about it the entire night, he'd tried to find a few ways to make it up to her.

****

Ginny spent ten times longer on her makeup than usual. The cut on her head had started to heal nicely and the bruise had faded to a less obvious color. The fit of her new white suit was better than she'd expected for coming off the rack. Her shoes and handbag were a perfect match. She felt well put together, as her sixth grade teacher would say. She hoped Brett would think so too. It would be the first thing she'd done right since crossing the Georgia state line.

At exactly four-fifteen, the front doorbell rang. Ginny wondered if the deputy picking her up would be one of the men who'd responded to her accident. She was pleasantly surprised when it wasn't. Instead, she found a female deputy. She was glad to see that her soon-to-be husband was an equal opportunity employer.

"Nice to meet you, ma'am." The tall thin redhead held her hand out to Ginny. "I'm Deputy Jackson, but you can call me Lisa. I do believe you're the prettiest bride I ever did see."

The compliment gave Ginny the extra measure of confidence she needed. "Thank you, Lisa. I insist you call me Ginny."

"Now do you have everything you need?" Lisa asked. "Something old, something new, something borrowed, something blue?"

Ginny laughed. "I have old and new covered, but I'm afraid I fell short on borrowed and blue."

"Well, that's just plain bad luck." Lisa thought for a moment. "I've got just the thing. My momma's blue handkerchief is in the car from when I took her to church last Sunday. You can borrow it to put in your little purse there. And don't you worry, she didn't use it. She just carries it to flutter. My momma is a true Scarlet O'Hara."

Lisa held out the small white box she'd been holding. "The chief asked me to give you this. He stopped and got it this morning, on his way in."

Ginny's heart leaped, knowing Brett had thought of her that morning. Then, she felt silly; it was probably nothing special.

The card on the box made her smile. It simply read: *Don't forget rule number one—B.*

Inside the box was the most exquisite white orchid Ginny had ever seen. That one perfect orchid meant more to Ginny then a room full of roses ever could. How had he guessed that about her? She hoped it was a good portent for their new relationship.

With ten minutes to spare, Ginny stepped out of Lisa's squad car in front of the courthouse. She reached up to make sure the orchid was still firmly placed in her hair over her right ear. Ginny opened the double doors at the top of the steps and started down the hallway.

A tall dark woman in a navy blue business suit got up from a bench along the wall.

"Excuse me, but are you Virginia Dearing?"

Ginny stopped and hesitated. She didn't want to be rude, but she also didn't want to be late...again.

"Yes, I am. Can I help you?"

"I'm Marsha Silverfeather." The woman held out her hand. "My husband asked me to witness your marriage today. I don't know if you remember, but I'm the person who sent you the letter offering you the teaching job. I've looked forward to meeting you."

"Oh, yes." Ginny shook Marsha's hand. "I can't tell you how much I appreciate the opportunity. I'm so excited to get started."

Marsha gave her a knowing look. "As excited as you are about this marriage? That's why I've been waiting to speak to you. My husband and I are on the Council of Elders. I know all about the deal you made with the chief. I have to tell you that my vote didn't go toward this idea at all."

Ginny's heart sank. She knew it showed on her face. All the insecurities she'd had regarding the situation floated back to the surface. "I really need this job. I know I'll be a good teacher, and I know you won't regret hiring me, I promise."

Marsha patted Ginny's hand. "I'm not worried about your teaching ability. Your resume and references were impeccable. I just don't want you to feel you have to get married in order to have the job. If you like, you can turn right around and walk out of here. I'd help you find a place to stay until you could put together a few paychecks for a permanent place of your own."

Ginny hesitated. She could have the job and not have to get married? Then she thought about Brett. He was a hard man, but he'd already put up with a lot of trouble from her. And he was the one who had taken her resume to the school board. She wouldn't be here if it hadn't been for him. Without the marriage he was certain he would lose his job and his job meant everything to him. Could she risk being the cause of him losing that job? He'd never forgive her, and for some unknown reason, that mattered a lot to Ginny.

Marsha interrupted her thoughts. "You just think about it for a few minutes. We'll go inside and get started, but if you decide to hightail it out of here, I'll bar the doors and back you up."

Ginny had no doubt Marsha would and could do just that.

****

Two men waited in the judge's chamber, but Ginny had eyes for only one.

Brett stood when she walked in. He looked incredibly handsome in the gray suit she'd seen in his closet. It appeared to be tailor-made to fit his broad shoulders and narrow waist. His shirt was snow-white and crisply starched. It was buttoned to his throat where a beaded band held a small hand-carved wooden eagle. His hair hung loose down his back with three narrow braids on either side to hold it out of his face. One braid on the right was decorated with gray feathers, or maybe they were silver. The man oozed sex appeal.

Brett's amber eyes bore into hers, but the only recognition he gave her was a slight nod.

The judge, Ben Silverfeather, cleared his throat as he came around the desk. He wore a long black robe and his hair was cut short with a few silver threads at the temples. Other than that, he looked a lot like Brett. It seemed as though looking at Ben she could see Brett, twenty years into the future. She liked what she saw.

Marsha leaned in to whisper in Ginny's ear. "Couldn't you just choke on all the testosterone in this room?"

Ginny suppressed a giggle as Marsha introduced her to her husband.

"We're very pleased to have you here in Three Trees, Ms. Dearing," Ben said. "You're saving my wife's life by taking the teaching position at the high school. Shoot, you're at least saving her sanity. You came through for her, right at the last minute. I hope it works out well for you."

Ginny smiled and offered her hand. "Thank you, sir, but I feel like she's the one that saved me. Positions are hard to come by these days."

Ben paused for a moment. "We feel that you're making an incredible sacrifice for the job, agreeing to marry this boneheaded bear. Are you sure you want to go through with this? We'd understand if you've had a change of heart."

Ginny looked over at Brett. He'd turned to the side and appeared to be engrossed with the wood grain on his uncle's desktop. Still, she could see that his brows were folded into a deep frown. He was grudgingly allowing her this last chance to back out of their deal.

"Are we ready to get started?" Ginny asked.

As Ben delivered the short, somber service, Brett held her hands lightly. Ginny didn't hear a single word Ben spoke. The only sound she heard was the rapid beat of her heart. Marsha nudged her when it was her turn to say I do.

Ginny realized Brett had never touched her before, not in any way. The way he held on to her hand felt right, like that was exactly where her hand fit best. A feeling washed over Ginny at that moment. She was doing the right thing, she had no doubt. This next year would change her life for the better.

The spell was broken when he turned her right hand loose to place the ring on the third finger of her left hand. It was an unusual ring, but lovely, and so like Brett. It was a band of white gold underlying a band of pale green jade. An eagle, like the one around his neck and the one on the knife sheath she had given him, was etched in the center. A larger ring that matched it was placed in her right hand. Ginny quivered with unexpected anticipation as she slid it onto Brett's outstretched finger.

"By the powers vested in me by the state of Georgia, I now pronounce you husband and wife."

Brett's cheek brushed hers as he leaned in to whisper in her ear. "You look amazing." He placed a light kiss on her temple, and then placed his forehead against hers. He added just one more word, "Wife." A camera flashed, startling them both.

Marsha laughed as she took another picture. "Sorry kids, but people aren't going to believe this without proof."

****

Brett stepped out of the SUV, removed his jacket, and rolled the sleeves up on his shirt. He wished Ginny would say something, anything. She hadn't even asked to turn on the siren or lights. Maybe he would have let her today. After all, it was their wedding day. She didn't look like a happy new bride, though. Perhaps she was nervous thinking he'd expect more from her than she was willing to give. And she'd be right, he did want more, but he'd made her a promise and he always kept his promises. After the thirty days, it would be back up for negotiation. But with the mood she was in now, he had a sinking feeling that his chances weren't good.

He walked around the car to open Ginny's door.

Ginny blinked and looked around. She was surprised to find herself sitting in the parking lot of a place called Big Bob's Barbeque and Steak House. She'd slipped into a funk and didn't know how long they'd been driving or what direction they'd gone.

Inside the restaurant were large wooden booths, wood paneled walls, and wood planked flooring. The air smelled of grilling meat and wood smoke. She wondered when the fire marshal had last inspected Big Bob's. The place was clean, though, and people seemed to be enjoying themselves.

A cheery waitress showed them to a booth in the corner. Fifteen minutes later, she returned with a steak and baked potato for Brett and the largest Cobb salad Ginny had ever seen. She couldn't even remember ordering it. Maybe Brett had ordered it for her.

She wanted to eat and feel normal, but she couldn't. A large ball of apprehension had already filled her stomach. Even Brett seemed to be playing with his food more than eating it. Ginny searched her mind for a pleasant subject to discuss. She'd about settled on discussing the weather when three small children bounded out of the back dining room. The two little girls and their slightly older brother let loose with squeals and shouts as they ran toward her table.

The girls piled into Brett's side of the booth, covering him in hugs and kisses. The boy stood at the end of the table. He excitedly described his progress with a video game she'd never heard of.

For the first time, Ginny saw Brett break into a wide smile and laugh.

"Aren't you kids going to say hello to your new aunt?" a male voice beside her said.

Ginny turned to look up at a thinner, younger version of Brett in khaki shorts and a Greenpeace T-shirt. He had to be Brett's younger brother, Jake.

"I hear congratulations are in order." Jake leaned down and kissed Ginny on the cheek. He held his hand out to Brett. "Good work, old man."

"Word travels fast," Brett replied.

"I just got a call from Mia at the paper." He turned to Ginny. "That's my wife, I'm Jake and these are our rug rats, Mark, Tina and Tammy." He turned back to Brett. "She just downloaded a picture from your wedding. You're front-page news again, big brother."

"Is that really necessary?" Brett asked.

"Hey, news is slow right now." Jake shrugged. "Besides, it's nice to be able to print good news for a change. This issue is going to sell like hot cakes. People are going to need to see it with their own eyes to believe it.

"I've got to get going, but would you mind keeping the kids busy for a few minutes while I pay the check?"

"Sure," Brett said as he jiggled the twin girls on each of his knees.

As soon as their father was out of hearing distance, one girl turned to Brett and said, "Can I have some bubblegum, Uncle Brett?"

The other girl snuggled into his side. "Me too, Uncle Brett, I promise to be good."

Brett looked at the boy silently standing with a pleading look on his face. Brett wiggled his hand into his pants pocket and came out with a hand full of change. He picked three quarters out and passed them to the boy. "There's a machine by the door. If you're careful, you can dodge your dad and get to it while he comes back for the girls."

The boy disappeared seconds before Jake got back.

"Where's Mark?"

"He said he'd meet you by the door." Brett

nuzzled each girl's neck.

"You didn't give them gum again, did you? It took days to get it out of their hair the last time."

"Absolutely not," Brett said, "I've learned my lesson."

Jake looked at Ginny, and then back at Brett. "How about helping me get these little ankle-biters buckled into their seats?"

"Sure." To Ginny he said, "I'll be right back."

After the children were settled, Jake asked, "Are the two of you fighting already?"

"Every day," Brett replied dryly, "except today. I don't know what the problem is. She's not eating or talking or anything."

"She did just get married with absolutely no one she knows in attendance," Jake speculated. "A wedding is a huge deal to a woman, you know."

"I don't think that's it. I haven't seen her make as much as a phone call since she's been here. She doesn't even talk about anyone from home. And she talks a lot, so it seems like someone's name would have come up."

Jake grinned. "Sounds like you need to get to know your bride a little better. Can a married man give you a little advice, brother?"

"At this point, I'll take all the advice I can get."

Jake opened his door and sat down behind the wheel. "Next time your woman is wearing a brand new, beautiful white suit, don't take her to a barbeque joint."

Brett watched Jake drive away with a smile on his face. He walked back inside to try to salvage the evening. Surely he could think of some way to cheer up his new wife. When he reached their table, he saw that Ginny's eyes were red and puffy. She was trying to hide it, but he knew she'd been crying.

"Let's go home." He threw a handful of money on the table. "I've got an idea."

Chapter Seven

Brett opened her car door and held out his hand to help her down to the ground. Ginny was surprised by the chivalrous gesture. She tingled all over when her hand slid into his. The emotional day had drained her energy. She was sure that was the cause of her extreme emotions.

"Let's go inside and get out of these fancy clothes," Brett said in a deep, calm voice.

Ginny couldn't hold back an astonished and indignant gasp.

Brett rolled his eyes. "Put on some jeans and sturdy shoes. I'll meet you out back when you're done." He paused. "You can bring Bear along if you feel you need protection."

Ginny dressed in jeans and a lightweight plaid blouse. She carefully hung up her white suit. The only casual closed shoes she owned were a pair of running shoes. On her way through the kitchen she placed her orchid in a small bowl of water on the center of the table.

Brett was waiting outside with an old straw cowboy hat in his hand and a black felt one on his head. His hair was back in its usual braid. Wearing faded jeans, a T-shirt and boots, he still made her breath hitch. He looked her up and down, nodded and placed the straw hat on her head.

"The bay mare is for you." He pointed out the two horses standing next to the fence. The bay wasn't as big as his gray dappled Arabian, but she was beautiful.

"Her name is Cin, short for Cinnamon. Mine is

named Havoc. No one rides Havoc but me. That's a rule." Brett said the last sentence sternly. "Have you ever ridden?"

"I spent a couple summers in Kentucky with a college friend. Her family had a stable. I learned to ride fairly well there."

"Okay," Brett said as he raised a brow, "let's see what you can do."

Bear decided chasing mice in the barn was more fun than chasing the horses across the field and through the woods. Brett let him stay behind to watch over the house.

Ginny handled the horse well at any speed Brett set. He was pleased she had a perfect seat and was gentle with the animal. She seemed relaxed and happy. Finally he'd found something they had in common. She looked as pleased to be outdoors on the back of a horse as he was.

They watered the horses by the lake, and then tied them to a bush, where the grass was high and green. He laid out a blanket in the shade and placed their saddles at one end. Next, he collected broken tree branches and twigs to build a fire in an old pit a safe distance from the trees.

"Why do we need a fire?" Ginny asked.

"We need all the elements." Brett motioned toward the lake, the sky, the ground, and back to the fire as he said, "Water, air, earth and fire."

"Is this a Native American thing?"

Brett lowered his head and shook it. It was becoming a gesture she recognized as him gathering patience. He did it a lot around her.

"Yeah, in your language this would be called a truth telling."

"What would your people call it?"

"A truth telling. Now will you pay attention?" Brett stretched out on the blanket with his head resting on his saddle. "Come down here and make yourself comfortable."

Ginny copied his pose, and then asked, "What's next?"

"I'm going to ask you a question and you have to answer it, honestly and completely. After that, I'll answer a question you have. What is said will stay here when we leave."

"What's your question?"

Brett turned his head to look at her. She'd never seen him look so serious.

"Why is it such a bad thing to be married to me? I know I'm no prize, but you look as if you've just received a death sentence."

Ginny thought for a long moment. "I don't know if it will be bad. I don't really know you. I just hadn't imagined myself being married to anyone, ever."

"Go on," Brett prompted.

Ginny sighed. "I don't have a good history with men in general. My father took off when I was ten, and then my mother had a string of crappy boyfriends. I ended up in a few lousy foster homes and then there were my own boyfriend issues. I seem to bring the worst out in men. Something about me just seems to make them angry. You of all people should understand that. I make you angry all the time. It's safer for me to just be alone."

Brett felt lead form in his stomach. How bad had it been for her? Did he really want to know? He turned onto his side and propped his head on his hand. A tear race down her cheek before she could wipe it away. The lump in his throat made it hard to speak. "Ginny, I'm not angry with you. I'm just impatient and frustrated trying to get used to you. I want to, but it's harder than I expected. I've been alone for a long time and sometimes I behave badly. I'm an ass that way. But there's one thing I always want you to remember...you're safe here. You're always safe with me."

After a few moments of silence, Ginny asked her question. "Brett, do you wish you had married Diana today?"

"No," Brett answered without hesitation. With all the talk around town he wasn't surprised she'd heard about his former engagement. "I started seeing Diana Rainflower just after I'd been elected Sheriff. She thought I was important. She lavished attention on me and made me feel like the center of the universe. She listened to all my dreams and said they were her dreams as well. Then one day, a modeling agent came through town on his way to New York from Miami. He told her he could get her on the front cover of the fashion magazines. I haven't seen her since. I was furious and humiliated. That was a year ago. I'm just glad it happened before things had gone too far between us. I never want to be in a situation where I'm that vulnerable again."

"You built this house for her." Ginny made it a statement rather than a question.

"No, this house was my dream, not hers. I built it for the family I'd dreamed of having. I don't think she ever shared that dream either."

Ginny played with the ring on her finger as she thought about what he'd said. She pictured him with his little twin nieces, slipping quarters to his nephew to buy forbidden gum. She thought about the empty rooms upstairs. Having a family was a dream to him because he'd never had one like hers. But he hadn't asked about that, so she didn't have to tell. She was glad she didn't have to, not yet anyway. Was she being fair to him by holding that back? Maybe not, but the day was ending too nicely to spoil. The sun was nearly down. They'd have to go back soon. She just wanted to ask him one more question.

"Brett, why did you choose these rings?"

He looked down at his own. "Do you like them?"

"Very much," she said. "But they're so unusual."

"They weren't meant to be wedding bands, but the pale jade reminded me of your eyes. I find your eyes very fascinating."

Ginny was thrilled by his compliment. "Did they come with the eagle already engraved on them?"

"No, that was my idea. The eagle is my totem. It watches over me and guides me." He settled back against his saddle. "I hoped it would remind you of me."

Ginny was having a hard time identifying the new feelings she had for Brett, but she knew they felt right. "Maybe if we watch, we'll see an eagle fly over us."

Brett grinned. He'd never seen an eagle in this area, but knowing Ginny, anything could happen.

The sun was peeking over the horizon when Brett woke to the sound of Havoc's nickering. He looked at the display on his cell phone, 6:30 a.m. He figured he must have slept for ten hours. That hadn't happened in a long time.

He wondered what Ginny's reaction would be when she woke to find herself wrapped around him. She'd fallen asleep first and he hadn't wanted to disturb her. After the first hour she tossed around a little making whimpering sounds. It worried him that the stress of the day might have caused her to have a bad dream. But once her head was laid over his heart, she'd settled down. Now she had one arm curled over his waist and her leg crossed over the top of his.

He brought his arm around her to lay their left hands side by side. His was so much larger, rougher and darker, but the rings they wore were the same. She was his wife, at least for a year. It felt strange that being married to Ginny didn't seem like a bad idea anymore. It would be interesting to see how the next year would turn out. Brett was actually looking forward to the adventure.

Yesterday he'd chosen an orchid for her from the flower shop window because it reminded him of her. It looked so soft and delicate and flawless. When she'd shown up at the courthouse with the flower in her hair, he knew he'd made the right choice, about everything. She'd been stunning in her white wedding suit and she was stunning now, cuddled at his side wearing blue jeans.

He thought about the things she'd said the night before. She'd had it tougher than he'd ever imagined. What kind of a man could ever mistreat such a sweet little kitten like her? He made a promise to the spirits that no one would ever be mean to her again, including himself. Nothing had ever torn at his heart the way her tears had. She'd cried yesterday in his office too. It broke his heart to see her cry because she was silent about it, like she didn't think anyone would care. He cared.

He wondered what it would be like if the circumstances were different. He tried to shake the thought away. A girl like her wouldn't have taken a second look at a mixed blood Indian from a Podunk southern town. She'd been desperate and he'd taken advantage of that. He had to remind himself that want was a waste of time. He'd learned the hard way, dreams don't really come true.

As the sun rose, so did the temperature. Beads of perspiration formed above her pouty lips. If he waited too long, her delicate skin might start to burn. Before he could wake her though, she turned her head into his side and scrubbed her face against his ribs. A chuckle escaped him. He hadn't been tickled in a long time. Yes, he decided, he'd like to wake up this way every morning.

Ginny had one eye squinted open and her hair was a mess. When she realized where she was, she scurried back away from him.

"What are you doing here?"

Brett chuckled again. "I figured it would be rude to leave you out here all alone. Besides that, I'm your husband. Where else should I be?"

She sat up and rubbed her hands over her face. "You should be making me coffee and finding me a bathroom."

"Sorry, Dove, you'll have to wait for the coffee and take to the bushes."

She stumbled behind a bush a few yards away. Brett was surprised he hadn't gotten an argument from her. She returned a few minutes later.

"I couldn't find a toothbrush back there."

He lowered his head and shook it. "Go down to the lake and use your shirt tail. I've got breath mints."

"Oh goody," she said as she walked toward the water. "Breakfast."

Back at the barn, Brett taught Ginny the proper way to saddle, unsaddle, groom and feed the horses. After they were turned out he started mucking the stalls.

"I can't believe someone would teach you to ride and not teach you how to care for your horse. Do you think you could do this by yourself if I wasn't able to be home?"

"Don't start getting all bossy with me, chief. I still haven't had my coffee and I'm hot, sweaty and," Ginny raised her arm and took a big sniff. "Whoa!"

Brett threw his pitchfork on top of the wheelbarrow. "Go get a shower. I'll make the coffee."

****

This shower was even better than the one Ginny had taken her first night here. The warm water soothed her sore muscles. It was a good kind of soreness, though, like every muscle was reminding her she was young and alive. She could ride more often now and maybe she'd start running in the mornings. She'd be safe anywhere with Bear along.

While Ginny blow-dried her hair in front of the mirror she noticed the ring on her finger. She'd actually done it. She was married. Brett Silverfeather was her husband. She'd awakened in his arms and it had felt really good.

She'd had the urge to reach up and kiss him, but he hadn't shown any sign of invitation. Now that she knew he was over Diana, there was a greater possibility of it happening one day. She could only hope.

Remembering what he had told her as they watched the fire, reminded her of what she'd admitted to him. Had she said too much? She didn't want him to see her as damaged goods. She'd hated the pity her caseworker had always shown. Pity didn't do anyone any good, especially self-pity. She'd decided that a long time ago.

By the time she'd returned to the kitchen, the aroma of fresh coffee was calling her. On the table were two plates of fluffy scrambled eggs and crisp bacon. Brett buttered toast at the counter beside a large silver box with a big white bow. It hadn't been there when she'd come in from the barn. He must have put it there while she'd showered.

"What's in the box?"

Brett kept his back to her. "It's a wedding present."

"But all I gave you was a hunting knife."

He turned to place the plate of toast in the center of the table, but he still didn't look her in the eye. He seemed embarrassed. "It's a war knife and I love it. Now, are you going to look in the box?"

She intended to test the weight of the box, but found it was really only a half box covering a shiny new microwave oven. Brett smiled when she squealed and jumped up and down.

"Oh Brett, it's perfect, you shouldn't have. No,

you should. I love it."

Brett grabbed her shoulders and turned her to look at him. "This is only to warm things or thaw them out. That's a new rule. I don't want my meals coming out of cardboard or plastic containers. Do you understand?"

The smile faded from Ginny's face. "You may have to get used to being hungry for a while. It'll take me some time to figure out the whole cooking thing."

Brett smiled again. His smile was every bit as devastating as Ginny had imagined it would be.

"Look inside. There's another gift in there...for both of us, I guess."

Ginny pressed the button on the front of the machine and the door sprang open. Lying inside was a big brand-new Betty Crocker cookbook. She decided right then and there, that Betty Crocker was going to be her new best friend.

"I love it!"

Ginny was thumbing through the new cookbook and chewing on a piece of toast when Brett's cell phone rang. He checked the display and flipped it open. She only heard him speak twice, "Hello," and a minute later, "I'll be right there." The next thing she knew he had his badge on a chain around his neck and his car keys in his hand.

Brett ran for his bedroom and Ginny followed. She watched as he unlocked a safe under his nightstand and pulled out his gun belt.

"What's going on?"

Brett fastened the heavy belt low around his jeans and looked up at her. "Do you remember the Harvey boys who blew up Mr. Crammer's henhouse?"

"They're children, Brett, you can't shoot them."

"First of all, you'd be surprised how dangerous a teenager can be. You'd better learn that and keep it in mind before you start teaching high school. Remember Columbine? Second, it's not the boys. They were the ones who called it in. Their old man, John, is holding their mom at gunpoint. He's drunk and mad, as usual, but I've known him for years and they're hoping I can talk him down. This time must be really bad if it has Kyle and Cole scared enough to call for help."

Ginny crossed her arms over her waist. Her delicious breakfast had suddenly turned into a huge rock in her belly. "Oh Brett, I don't know if I can handle this."

Brett grabbed her upper arms and made her look up at him. "Listen to me, Dove. This is what I am. You have to decide if that is something you can live with and you have to decide soon. Right now, Peggy Harvey needs me. I'll be back as soon as I can."

Ginny watched Brett drive away and then went back to the kitchen. Both of their breakfast plates were still half full. She scraped them into Bear's bowl and called him in from the backyard. She'd feel better having Bear close by. Wasn't it funny how things had changed so quickly?

Chapter Eight

Ginny sat at her kitchen table turning the pages of her new cookbook. She didn't look down to see a single picture or read a word. She stared into space with nothing on her mind but Brett. He'd said this Harvey man had a gun and he was drunk. He was crazy enough to have the gun pointed at his wife, terrifying his own sons.

She'd known from the beginning Brett was a sheriff, but she hadn't considered the danger he would sometimes face. Here was a man she'd never laid eyes on a week ago, and now she was absolutely terrified of losing him. How did other women handle having lawmen for husbands? He was right; she had to learn to live with it, at least for a year. The best thing to do right now was put it out of her mind.

Ginny wished desperately for someone she could talk to. She'd left a few friends in Michigan, but she couldn't talk to them yet. What would she say? "I know I only left six days ago, but I got married yesterday and my husband has left me at home alone in order to face down a man with a gun." Yeah, that would go over like a concrete blimp.

Today was the first real day of their marriage. She resolved to make the best home cooked meal Brett had ever come home to.

Ginny thought about calling his mother to find out what he liked best. But what if she asked where he was? She wouldn't be able to lie to Mrs. Silverfeather. There was no sense in worrying her as well. She'd just have to go through what he'd stocked in the freezer and figure it out.

****

Brett was surprised to find Officer Bryant and another man from the highway patrol crouching behind an old pickup with his two deputies, Lisa Jackson and Beau Stevens. Calls in this area were in the GHP jurisdiction, but they usually liked to leave the domestic cases to the local authorities.

"How's that pretty little fiancée of yours, chief?" Bryant asked when Brett settled beside him.

Brett smiled. "She's my wife now and we're getting along. The knife she was carrying that day was my wedding present."

"Nice," Bryant replied, "what did you get her, an AK-47 assault rifle?"

"Nope, I gave her a microwave oven."

Bryant shook his head. "Take it from a married man, chief. You never give a woman a gift that goes in the kitchen or has an electrical cord. They want things that are sexy or sentimental."

"He's right, chief," Lisa confirmed.

"Okay, I admit it," Brett held up his hands, "I bought her a cookbook too. It was an act of self-defense. The woman is lethal in the kitchen."

Brett raised himself up enough to see the house through the trucks missing side windows. "What's the situation here?"

"The two boys are in the back of my car, out by the road," Bryant answered. "I was afraid to leave them loose in case something serious happens. According to them, the old man woke up still half drunk. He wanted eggs for breakfast. The wife told him a snake had gotten into the henhouse and it had eaten all the eggs. That just pissed him off."

The second GHP officer spoke up. "The man must really like eggs."

"Okay," Brett said as he stood up.

"Hey, John, can you hear me in there?" He shouted, "It's Brett Silverfeather."

"Yeah, I hear you chief, what do you want?" a voice from inside the house yelled back.

"I was thinking of going over to Betty's café for breakfast. You want to go along? I'm buying."

There was silence for several minutes and then the voice yelled out again. "Betty makes some pretty good eggs. I think I will."

The door slowly opened and John Harvey stepped out onto the porch. He was dirty and unkempt. His hairy chest and arms hung out from around a pair of worn-out denim overalls. The thirty-eight special in his hand hung limply at his side.

"I don't think Betty allows any guns in the place." As soon as the words were out of his mouth his young deputy, Beau, stood up to take a look. He turned back in time to see John Harvey raise his gun.

Brett had reached his deputy and shoved him back behind the old truck just before a loud crack pierced the air and a bolt of lightning shot through the back of his left shoulder. Before he passed out, Brett heard two more cracks even closer.

****

Ginny inhaled the aroma of the peach cobbler as she slid it out of the oven. She'd found the peaches in the bottom drawer of the refrigerator along with the fresh corn which was now shucked and waiting to be boiled. Two thick pork chops were thawing and she'd already made the pecan stuffing for them. It's amazing what you can learn from books.

While turning off the oven, Ginny noticed the clock on the back of the stove. Brett had been gone for almost four hours. She supposed all the booking and fingerprinting stuff took time, but why did it have to be today? This was her first day of married life.

There was a knock on the front door. Ginny

couldn't imagine who it could be. Brett and his family all seemed to use the back door. Walking through the dining room toward the living room, Ginny hoped it wasn't a salesman. They always took her as a soft touch and were hard to get rid of. The knocking came again, louder and more urgent. She was going to give this guy a piece of her mind.

Deputy Lisa Jackson stood on the front porch. She wasn't smiling like she had the day before. As a matter of fact, she looked extremely pale. Ginny's knees began to wobble and her heart pounded like the hooves of a herd of mustangs.

"Grab your purse, the chief's been shot."

****

In the waiting room outside of the surgical unit Ginny was greeted by the night crew deputies, Carl and Larry, along with the night dispatcher, Pamela Armstrong. They told her they'd been called by, Cora Marshall, the daytime dispatcher.

"Don't you worry, Ms. Silverfeather," Carl said, "your family's on the way."

Ginny didn't know what made her feel stranger, being called Ms. Silverfeather, being accepted by her husband's men, or hearing she had a family coming to support her. It was all overwhelming.

One man hadn't risen to greet her, but he wore a deputy's uniform like the rest. He was younger than the others and smaller. His hat was propped against his side while he ran his fingers through his dark curly hair. Lisa knelt in front of him with a cup of water. Ginny guessed he was Beau Stevens, the second deputy on duty that morning. Lisa had filled her in on everything that had happened on their way into town. She knew he must be riddled with guilt for his mistake. Ginny wouldn't have wanted to be in his shoes, then or now.

"This is my fault," the young man moaned. "The chief had everything under control before I screwed up. I can't believe I got him shot. I'll never forgive myself. I'm handing my badge in as soon as this is over."

Poppy walked in just in time to hear Beau's declaration. He stepped in front of the young deputy. "A man learns more from his mistakes than he does from any amount of training. Those are the lessons that stay with him for a lifetime. If I were to choose the man to have at my grandson's back, I would now choose you."

"I don't think the chief is going to see it that way, Poppy," Beau replied.

"We'll see." Poppy sat and opened a magazine.

The next person to arrive was Mrs. Silverfeather. She wrapped Ginny into a hug. "Have you spoken to the doctor yet?"

"They're still in surgery," Ginny replied.

Mrs. Silverfeather took a seat and pulled a large ball of yellow yarn and two knitting needles out of her hobo bag. "The other children are building a fire up on the ridge. They'll take care of the spirits while we keep an eye out here. Don't worry, Dove, the spirits have always favored Brett. He's a strong warrior."

Time crept by as the project on Mrs. Silverfeather's lap grew larger. Ginny was fascinated by the way the woman could knot the yarn together to make such a perfect and beautiful blanket, probably for the baby Nina was expecting. Nina and Julie had probably learned the craft at her knee.

Ginny couldn't imagine her own mother doing such a thing. She couldn't imagine her mother taking the time to comfort her with a hug the way Brett's mother had. Her mother, Joyce Dearing, had always been more interested in having the attention focused on herself, especially male attention. Thinking about her mother made Ginny's stomach feel sour.

A doctor walked into the room. It seemed as though the air had been sucked out. Everyone turned silent and still. He walked straight up to Brett's mother. "I have good news, Mrs. Silverfeather."

Brett's mother reached for Ginny's hand. "Dr. Carlisle, this is Brett's new wife. You should speak to her."

She turned to Ginny. "Dr. Carlisle removed my gallbladder last year. He's a good man."

"Thank you, Mrs. Silverfeather," the doctor said, "It's nice to meet you, Mrs. Silverfeather. I mean, umm..."

"You can call me Ginny."

The doctor smiled and continued. "Anyway, Ginny, no major organs or arteries were involved. I swear that man must have an angel on his shoulder."

"Something like that," Brett's mother quipped.

The doctor smiled again. "Of course, we'll have to watch for infection and keep his arm immobile for a while, but the chief should be able to go home in a few days. I'll be checking on him, but Dr. Baxter will take over now. He should be settled in his room in about fifteen minutes or so. Visiting time is between the hours of 1 and 8 p.m. Of course, that doesn't apply to you, Mrs....Ginny."

Ginny thanked the doctor, hugged her mother-in-law and had a little time to freshen herself up in the ladies' room before seeing Brett.

When she reached his door, the curtain around his bed had been pulled to hide him from strangers walking past in the hallway. She was surprised to hear his voice. "Put your badge back on, deputy, you still have two hours left on your shift and I expect you to be there again tomorrow."

"But I nearly got you killed, Chief," Beau

Stevens said.

"Had you had a drink before arriving at the Harvey place?" Brett asked.

"No sir."

"Did you at any time fire your weapon?"

"It never left my holster. You know that, Chief."

"Well, John Harvey did both of those things. He's the one I'm blaming for this," Brett explained. "You made a mistake because of inexperience. Now you have the experience to keep it from happening again."

She heard the young deputy moan, "You saved my life, Chief. He was aiming right at me. I'll never forget that."

Brett's voice gentled. "I'd take a bullet every day of the week before I'd let anyone take down one of my men, but you can keep that to yourself."

"Yes sir. Thank you, Chief."

When Beau passed Ginny at the door he nodded sheepishly and kept walking.

Ginny forced a big smile and walked into Brett's room. She sat down in a chair on the left side of his bed. It scared her to see how pale he looked.

"New rule, Chief," she said past the lump in her throat. "No more getting shot."

He shot her an innocent look. "You act like I did it on purpose."

"You'll do anything to avoid my cooking."

"Maybe," he smiled, "but now we'll get to see how well you can take care of the horses without me."

His last two words echoed in her mind, *without me*. Those words triggered Ginny's breaking point. She laid her head down on the edge of his mattress and shattered into a million tiny pieces. She couldn't control the sobs tearing out of her chest or the tears soaking his sheet.

Brett was surprised, overjoyed and a little

uncomfortable with her reaction. Hell, he didn't know how he felt. He ran the fingers of his right hand through her silky blonde hair. "It's all right, Dove. Everything's going to be all right."

Ginny pulled two tissues from a box at the side of his bed, blew her nose, and wiped at her red eyes. "I've been wondering why everyone has started calling me Dove."

"Because Poppy says so. He had a dream, months ago. He saw my eagle and a white dove flying side by side. He says it was a vision of my future and the first time he laid eyes on you, he knew it was you. You're my Dove."

Ginny sniffled. "That's so beautiful."

"It is, and so are you." Brett wrapped his hand around the nape of her neck and drew her closer. Ginny melted into the softest, warmest, most perfect kiss of her life.

Poppy and Mrs. Silverfeather stood outside the door. The curtain was still drawn, but they'd heard every word. They had no doubt what was currently going on. Poppy took his daughter-in-laws arm and whispered, "Maybe we should give them a few minutes."

Chapter Nine

Ginny visited Brett at the hospital on Saturday
and Sunday, but the room had been crowded with
friends, neighbors, family, cops from every law
enforcement branch and other emergency
responders. Essentially, every adult within a fifty-
mile radius came through his room. They hadn't had
a single moment alone since they shared their first
kiss on Friday night. They'd barely made eye
contact. Neither of them knew what to say to the
other. Neither of them knew that it had been the
only thing on the other's mind.

The hospital staff was almost as annoyed as
Brett by the constant flow of visitors. Visiting hours
were bad enough, but law enforcement officers and
emergency personnel were allowed the run of the
hospital at all hours. No one could get any rest, least
of all the patient.

Everyone had finally been run out of the room
on Sunday evening when Dr. Baxter walked in to
check Brett's wound.

"You've got to get me out of here, Doc," Brett
groused. "I haven't had two consecutive hours of
sleep since Friday morning. If you don't sign my
release tonight, this is going to turn into a murder
suicide situation."

"Yeah, I've heard all about it from the nurses,"
Dr. Baxter laughed. "They say you're more popular
than Brad Pitt in the nude at a sorority house
luncheon. Now Chief, I've known you for ten years
and I know I can't trust you to take your medication.
Also, you're hardly in any position to keep these

bandages changed. But one thing's for certain, something has to be done. The staff is threatening to walk out if I don't get this floor under control."

Brett leaned forward and winced. "I'll do anything to sleep in my own quiet, soft, big bed, anything. You're looking at a desperate man."

"Yeah, I got that idea when you threatened to kill me." The doctor thought for a few minutes before he continued. "Okay, I'll let you go, but you have to agree to follow three rules, and I mean to the letter. First, you have to take a full series of antibiotics on time until they're gone. If you get an infection, it'll be a long time before you see sunlight again. Second, no use of that injured arm, it stays in a sling at all times, even when you're sleeping. You can prop it on a pillow. And last but definitely not least, no Ginny. I know you just got married, but things could get out of control in a moment of passion and you could pull out all of Dr. Carlisle's fancy stitching. Then you'll be in here for so long, you'll get a permanent, fluorescent light tan."

"I'll do it," Brett said with enthusiasm. "Call Ginny and tell her to come back with a pair of jeans. I'll be out of here so fast you'll only see my vapor trail."

****

Ginny woke on Monday morning, Labor Day, to the sounds of Bear barking, doors thumping, and Brett cursing. She stumbled into the hall and tried to decide which way to go first; across to the bathroom, to the left where Bear waited to be let out, or to the right where Brett seemed to be having a temper tantrum, or as it was better known in the south, a tizzy fit.

"Both of you just shut up!" she yelled. It was time they realized she wasn't a morning person. To Ginny's satisfaction, the house suddenly fell silent. She felt all powerful.

First, Ginny did a quick step to the back door to let Bear out. If she ended up having to clean up a mess, she'd rather it be her own. Once her own most urgent needs were met, she tapped on Brett's bedroom door. She felt much better and spoke in a sweeter and quieter tone. "May I come in?"

"I don't know," Brett snapped, "do you plan to turn the knob or just kick the door down?"

"You're safe with me."

Or maybe not. When she opened the door, she caught her breath in a gasp. Brett stood in the center of the room. The only things he was wearing were his arm sling and a pair of black boxer briefs. The tight, stretchy garment dipped low in the front due to the nice way he filled them out. She honestly tried to look him in the eye, but on her way up, her attention was caught by the expanse of dark smooth skin over washboard abs and a wide strong chest. The man was Playgirl centerfold ready.

Brett cleared his throat. "A little help here, please? I can't get my britches on one-handed."

Ginny was confused until she saw the uniform pants in his right hand. He needed help dressing and she couldn't think of who to call. Suddenly it hit her. She was his wife. He expected her to help. Would this fall into the category of for better, or for worse? And what was he doing with his uniform anyway? He'd left the hospital less than twelve hours ago.

"Why are you out of bed?"

"I got lonely," Brett smirked. "Are you volunteering to keep me company in there? I'd be glad to crawl back in, in exchange for some serious body heat. Who knows," he winked, "it could be mutually satisfying."

A wave of heat overtook her entire body as her imagination kicked into overdrive. What was wrong with her? She'd never had erotic fantasies until she got to Three Trees. Perhaps it was caused by something in the water. She should have it bottled and sell it to make a fortune.

"You know I have to go to the school today," she croaked. Embarrassed, she cleared her throat. "It's my last chance to check out my classroom before the kids arrive tomorrow."

Brett took a step closer. "Hmmm, I didn't hear a no in there anywhere."

"You were just shot three days ago." Ginny looked as panicked as the only girl bunny in a full hutch. "I thought you'd still be heavily medicated and resting for a while."

"I'm not taking those pain pills," Brett stated matter-of-factly, "I need to be alert. The county doesn't pay me to lie on my back. Instead, I plan to sit on my butt at my desk."

"Well then, you can just go to work naked."

Brett glowered at her. "I don't have to. Lisa is picking me up this morning. If you won't help me get dressed, she will."

"Like hell." Ginny jerked the pants out of his hand.

Brett grinned. "Careful, Dove. That almost sounded like jealousy."

"Shut up."

She knelt in front of him and held his pants open as he gripped her shoulder with one hand and stepped into them. Her head was turned to the side and her eyes were squeezed shut. She was leaned back at a dangerous angle.

"You have seen men before, haven't you?"

"Of course," Ginny said.

"Then you know there isn't anything down there that bites."

Ginny stood, picked up a rolled pair of socks and threw them at his head. He ducked successfully.

She had his socks and shoes on, and then his

undershirt and uniform shirt. When she finished buttoning it, he asked, "Is it smooth in the back? Tuck it in tight. Just run your hand down in there."

Ginny gave him a horrified look.

Brett laughed. "Then maybe you should check the front."

"You're asking for the worst wedgie in history, Chief."

"Okay, okay," he conceded, "just get my gun belt then."

"You've got to be kidding."

He shrugged his good shoulder. "I'm right handed. It shouldn't be a problem."

"Who do you plan to shoot?"

"You, if you give me any more trouble."

Ginny braided Brett's hair extra tight, made his coffee extra strong, and served him a bowl of lumpy oatmeal. He'd learn not to threaten her.

****

The day didn't get any easier when Ginny saw her classroom was an old mobile unit which had been used as storage for the last few years and had recently been emptied. She lugged in what janitorial equipment she could find from the main building and began scrubbing the floor and cabinets. She found several long folding tables and chairs in a room behind the gymnasium. She set them up in rows to use in place of the missing desks. The textbooks that had been left in a box by the door were old and worn. The supply closet was empty and Ginny mentally calculated how much money was left of her savings, not much. This would have to be a bare-bones operation.

The room had become as hot as the inside of an oven. The thermostat was no help. She went outside. As hard as she banged on the one small air conditioning unit, she couldn't make it turn on. It would definitely require a power greater than herself, and so she walked to the administration office.

The lobby was cool, quiet, and totally deserted, but she heard a computer printer rattling from one of the back offices. "Hello?" she called.

A moment later a short, plump middle-aged woman stepped up to the counter that divided the offices from the main part of the room. The woman was wearing a brown skirt that reached several inches below her knees, a pink floral blouse, buttoned to her throat and her graying brown hair in a tight bun at the back of her neck. She looked grandmotherly except for the sour expression she wore.

Ginny held out her hand. "Hi. I'm Virginia Dearing, I mean Silverfeather. Please, call me Ginny."

The woman gave Ginny's hand a disgusted look and turned up her nose. "I'm Henrietta Dagget, the vice principal." She said her name as if it should be familiar to Ginny. "You may call me Mrs. Dagget. What is it you need Mrs. Silverfeather?" She said Silverfeather as if the word offended her.

"Well, Mrs. Dagget, it's very nice to meet you. I'm sorry for my appearance, but my room needed a lot of cleaning. The reason I came in, is because my air conditioner doesn't seem to work. I wonder if we could have someone look at it."

Mrs. Dagget's face turned red as she tightened her lips. "I should have expected you to wait until the last minute, on a holiday no less, to come in here with complaints and demands. It must be convenient to have connections at the school board, but that'll get you nowhere with me. You'll study our policies and follow them to the letter. Also, I'll expect a complete lesson plan from you by the end of this week."

Ginny couldn't hold back her irritation. "I'm

sorry I haven't been by sooner, Mrs. Dagget, but I just arrived in town a week ago. Since then I've gotten married and my husband has been in the hospital after being shot. I've been extremely busy, but I've already completed a lesson plan and I'd be happy to read over the school policies. Now about the air conditioner-"

"Oh yes," Mrs. Dagget interrupted with a menacing gleam in her eye. "I know all about your husband and everything you've been up to since getting into town. Let me tell you now that Three Trees is a small, quiet community. People here won't put up with shenanigans from their schoolteachers. And as far as your husband is concerned, maybe the next sheriff will do a better job. It's time the Silverfeathers found out they don't run this town."

Ginny suddenly felt like a mother lion protecting a new cub. "Mrs. Dagget, no one could do a better job protecting this town than my husband."

"I believe the new sheriff will," Mrs. Dagget sneered, "and that man will be *my* husband, Orville Dagget. In a couple of months, Brett Silverfeather will be looking for a new job. I'm sure his family can come up with something for him, unless he leaves town with his tail between his legs."

Mrs. Dagget's smarmy smile was even more disturbing than her sneer.

To the surprise of both women, another office door opened. A large blond man in tan slacks, a white shirt and wire framed glasses appeared. "You must be Ginny. It's so nice to have you here. My name is Clive Winters. Please, call me Clive. I'm the principal here. Welcome to Three Trees High School. It sounds like you're ready to get started."

Ginny gave him a wide smile and then turned it on Mrs. Dagget with a lifted brow. The principal had heard every word through his office door.

Clive continued, "We'll have the air conditioner

fixed for you by tomorrow, won't we, Mrs. Dagget? We're all going to do everything we can to see you're happy here. Your husband and I have been friends since kindergarten. He was my best receiver on our football team. My cousin Cora is one of his dispatchers. Hell of a man, Brett. I intend to give him my vote again this year."

Ginny smiled and shook Clive's hand, but if looks could kill, Mrs. Dagget would have been charged with murder. Ginny knew that this fight was a long way from over.

"I appreciate it, Clive, and I'll be sure to tell Brett he has your support."

****

It was one o'clock and Ginny was still steaming mad over her confrontation with Mrs. Dagget. She wondered if she should tell Brett about it, but she didn't want him to get the idea she was already having problems in her new job. After all, this job was the reason she'd come all the way to Three Trees. This job was why she'd married a virtual stranger, even if he was the hottest man she'd ever seen.

While sitting at one of the two traffic lights on Main Street, Ginny saw Poppy a block away. He was leaving the hardware store and crossing the street to *Hooligan's Bar & Grill*. She smiled. Hooligan was a word as old-fashioned as shenanigans. Could this town get any more quaint?

Poppy had been a good listener the first time they met. He'd be the perfect person to talk to now. Maybe they could even have lunch together. It would save her from her own cooking and maybe give her a little insight on how to handle Henrietta Dagget.

She pulled into the small parking lot. The only other vehicle there was a Jeep with tires that stood taller than her car and a gun rack across the back window. She couldn't remember seeing it before, and it would have been hard to miss.

Inside, it took a moment for her eyes to adjust to the dimmer lighting. Immediately, though, she heard boisterous laughter at the bar. It seemed that two men and a woman were still celebrating the long holiday weekend. They had a line of beer bottles and shot glasses in front of them and they looked as though they hadn't bathed or changed clothes in several days, maybe weeks. Ginny assumed they'd been hunting and camping.

Poppy and the bartender were the only other people currently in the bar. Ginny quietly circled the room to avoid attracting the drunken group's attention and sat across from Poppy at a small round table by the kitchen door.

"You look a little down, Dove. A newlywed bride should be smiling."

"It hasn't been easy fitting in, Poppy," Ginny said. "People here are strangers and I can't seem to figure out who my enemies are until I'm under attack. Did you know Brett's opponent for the sheriff's position is married to the vice principal of my school?"

"I wouldn't worry about her," Poppy said. "Everyone knows what an old sourpuss Henrietta is. I swear the woman gargles with vinegar. Clive won't let her bother you. He's a good man. If you have trouble, just let him know."

The redheaded owner of Hooligan's, Sean Riley, approached with a white apron tied around his generous waist and set down a couple of glasses filled with ice-cold tea. He pulled a note pad and a stubby pencil from his shirt pocket. "Will you be having the usual today, Poppy?"

"You bet," Poppy answered. "Your chili is what keeps my old heart pumping. My daughter-in-law thinks I should be eating rabbit food all the time. It's a hell of a way for a man to live out the last days of his life."

"Now, Poppy, you know you'll probably outlive all of us," Sean said. "You've got to be the healthiest man in town."

Poppy smiled. "I know, but if I say things like that it makes the ladies want to cuddle up to me more. And speaking of ladies, Sean, have you met my new granddaughter, Ginny?"

"So this is the chief's new bride." The bartender gave Ginny a soft smile. "I should have recognized you from the picture in yesterday's paper. That was quite a headline. 'Sheriff Shot Within Hours of Wedding.' You looked right pretty in that picture, too."

"I didn't realize I was a celebrity." Ginny laughed as she held out her hand. "I was so busy worrying about Brett I must have missed seeing the paper."

"Don't worry about it," Poppy said. "Brett's mother, Emma, picked up a half dozen copies. She has one put away for you."

"How's the chief doing?" Sean asked.

Ginny had a sudden picture in her mind of Brett in his underwear. She smiled. "He's doing great. Thanks for asking."

Sean licked the tip of his pencil. "What'll you have for lunch? I don't want to be away from the bar too long with those out-of-towners getting so rowdy. After this round, I'm cutting them off. I have a bad feeling about them."

Ginny understood. She couldn't tolerate being around drunks. She'd had too much experience with it as a young girl. "Why don't you pick something for me that's quick and simple, but a little milder than chili. I've had a very long, hot morning."

"You've got it." Sean winked. He nudged Poppy. "I think she's a keeper."

As soon as Sean disappeared into the kitchen,

the rowdy trio turned their attention on Poppy and Ginny.

"Well, look what we've got here." A tall skinny man with a mullet haircut and holey T-shirt staggered toward them. "It's an old Indian and his little blonde squaw. We'd better circle the wagons, folks." He giggled then added, "I don't think you can handle this young girl, gramps. Maybe I should take her off your hands."

The fat, dark haired man with a grizzly beard and a John Deere baseball cap followed. He grabbed his crotch and laughed. "I wouldn't mind taking a turn at her myself." He slammed a bottle of beer on their table. "Have a little firewater, old man. This shouldn't take long."

When the first man grabbed Ginny by the wrist and tried to pull her out of her chair, she picked up the beer bottle and hit him in the shoulder with it.

The skinny woman with dark rooted blonde hair and Daisy Duke shorts flew at her from the other side. "You better leave your hands off my brother, lady, and don't even think of trying to take my man. I seen you start flirting with him the minute you walked in the door." She grabbed a fistful of Ginny's hair and pulled.

Ginny rounded on her with a punch that knocked out the woman's front tooth. They fell to the floor and were still clawing and punching when Brett walked in with Lisa Jackson.

He saw that Sean had the skinny man pinned against the wall with a chair, like a lion tamer. His grandfather sat on the fat man's chest with an old steak knife to his throat. And Brett's very own wife had a headlock on a woman who was drooling blood.

"For the love of Pete, what's going on here?" Brett shouted.

"This crazy Indian is trying to scalp me!" the fat man shouted.

The skinny man must have noticed Brett's uniform and skin color. "Shut the hell up, Lloyd."

"I was only offering him a shave," Poppy said innocently.

"Blondie here was trying to steal my man," the woman slurred as she squirmed out from under Ginny and staggered to her feet.

Brett turned the skinny man against the wall so Lisa could handcuff him.

Just as he handed her his own cuffs for the second man, Sean spoke up. "They were trying to force themselves on your wife, Chief."

"They did what?" Brett grabbed the fat man by his hair and slammed his face into the wall. It made a wet smacking noise and the man came away with a deluge of blood down his mouth and chin. The skinny man in cuffs tried to run, but Brett broke a chair across his back. Amazingly he'd done it all with one hand.

"Get hold of yourself, Chief," Lisa warned him.

Brett said to Lisa, "Have Bernie come and pick up that piece of crap Jeep for impound. These three are going to sleep it off in my jail." Then he turned to Poppy. "Take my wife home. Tell her to stay put until I get there."

"I'm standing right here, Brett." Ginny held her torn shirt together.

"Don't blame her," Poppy said. "She was defending herself...and doing a fine job of it, too."

"You're damned lucky I'm not throwing you in jail along with these filthy idiots, Poppy."

Once the others cleared away, he said to Ginny, "I asked you here to save my job. That may be the biggest mistake I ever made. After this, I'll be lucky if I'm not run out of town with tar and feathers."

Ginny walked out behind the others without another word. Again, she hadn't thought her day could get worse, but it had just reached a record low.

Chapter Ten

Ginny had tried to soften Brett's temper with a pot of spaghetti and a fresh garden salad for dinner. It had proven to be another mistake. She quickly found out you shouldn't make spaghetti for a man with one arm in a sling. After a few feeble attempts at twirling the spaghetti around his fork, he cut the pasta into tiny pieces and scooped it into his mouth. To Brett's credit, he didn't complain once. Actually, he didn't speak a word during the entire meal.

Ginny sneaked glances at Brett while she tended the animals. He had an apple for each of the horses hidden in his sling. While Cin and Havoc each ate their treats, he rubbed their necks and cooed sweet compliments to them. Ginny wished he could treat her as nicely as he did his four-legged friends. Her chances of any kind of friendliness from Brett grew even slimmer when she accidentally tipped the wheelbarrow and covered his left boot in horse manure. This just wasn't her day.

Brett calmly shook off the excess manure and walked to the back porch. He toed the boots off over the side of the porch and walked inside in his socks. He sat on the sofa and read while Ginny ironed her blouses and watched him through the kitchen door. He didn't make a sound or turn a page. She would have given anything to know what he was thinking.

Finally he put his book down and returned to the kitchen. "I guess I need help changing this bandage, but if you'd rather not do it, I can call my mother to come over."

Ginny was getting extremely annoyed by his

passive behavior.

"That won't be necessary," she said, "I'm sure everyone has heard about all my faux pas by now. There's no need to point them out for your mother."

Ginny's arms circled his waist for a moment to pull the shirt from his pants. Damn, he loved the way she smelled. Brett watched her fingers undo every button. After the shirt was gone, her hands slid up his body to lift his white undershirt over his head. He didn't care about the bandage she pulled away, or the sting of the ointment she applied. All he could think about were her hands stroking his skin. She gently smoothed the fresh bandage into place and then bent to pick up the remaining supplies. By the time she was finished, he was as hard as a cigar store wooden Indian. Being dressed by a beautiful woman was great, but being undressed by said woman was earthshaking.

Ginny stood back and folded her arms. "Is there anything else you need?"

Brett quickly calculated in his head. Twenty-two days left of the thirty he'd promised her. If he was ever going to get anywhere with his wife, he'd have to find a way to get along with her. He picked up his discarded shirts and stood. "No, I'm tired. I'll just go to bed now."

****

On Tuesday morning Brett quietly stood as Ginny helped him dress. She missed the jokes and innuendos from the morning before. When she asked what he'd like for breakfast he finally spoke.

"I'll pick something up in town." He headed toward the door.

"You aren't going to drive, are you?" Ginny asked, alarmed.

"Lisa is picking me up. I'll wait for her on the front porch."

"I'm going to the school early today. I could drop

you off on my way," Ginny offered.

"No thanks," he said with his back to her.

There was a buzz of silence in the house when the door closed behind him. Ginny blinked back tears. Her relationship with her new husband was like a rollercoaster of emotions and like other rollercoaster rides, it was making her feel sick.

She refused to let the turmoil between them ruin the first day of her new job. She intended to greet her students with a smile on her face. She might not be much of a wife, but she planned to be the best teacher Three Trees High School ever had.

****

A large glass window in Brett's office overlooked the bullpen. That's what they called the lobby area where his deputies and dispatcher were separated into cubicles, quietly working on reports. They'd be going home now that the day shift had come in to relieve them.

Since the incident at the Harvey place, Beau Stevens had been working harder than ever. Brett was confident he'd be the best cop out of all of them after he'd matured a little more. Maybe one day he'd even be sheriff.

Brett loved his position as sheriff. He'd felt a strong sense of protectiveness for the people he loved, especially after his father's death. That circle of loved ones had grown to include the whole town. They were his people, his extended family. He didn't really care about the badge or guns or glory, he just wanted to keep everyone safe. He'd had confidence in his ability to do so...until Ginny came along. How could a man ever admit that one little woman scared the life out of him?

Yesterday, when he found out his own wife had nearly been assaulted by two men right there in his own town, he suffered a moment of insanity. If it hadn't been for his deputy, he would have torn those men into a million pieces. It wasn't Ginny's fault it happened, but it was safer to put distance between them then to allow himself to get more emotionally attached to her.

It was bad enough that the sight of her made his libido jump into overdrive, but it was more than that. Her smile made his heart skip a beat. Her laughter made him feel content. Her scent made him feel at home. The touch of her hand comforted him. And her kiss, that one perfect kiss...

It wasn't supposed to be this way. She'd been a means to an end.

A small town like Three Trees wouldn't be able to hold a woman like her very long. She was meant for better things. She'd be gone in a year. And then what? He didn't want to miss her. He didn't want to have a hole ripped out of the middle of his life.

The phone rang. When he looked up, Beau had answered it.

Why was Beau the only person in the bullpen? Every desk should have been filled at this time of day. Where had the rest of his crew gotten off to?

Brett picked up his coffee cup and stepped out to get a refill. The coffee machine sat next to the doorway of their one and only interrogation room. He paused when he heard laughter inside.

"Yeah," Carl Sights was saying, "she's a di-rect descendant of Calamity Jane. Maybe we should start calling her Calamity Ginny."

Then Larry Graham spoke. "I'm not sure I'd even recognize her without blue lights flashing in her face."

Lisa Jackson added, "Speaking of faces, you should have seen the chief's when he found her rolling around on the floor with that drunken barfly yesterday. She'd actually knocked the woman's front tooth out. You gotta admit, the lady packs a punch."

"Makes you wonder what the chief's home life is

like now," Larry laughed. "We'd better send him home with a Kevlar vest and boxing gloves."

"Maybe we should see about having a private cell added on to the jailhouse." It was Carl again. "Lisa, you can make a quilt and ruffled curtains for it. We could make it like a little suite and call it Ginny Jail."

The two dispatchers, Pamela Armstrong and Cora Marshall, were breathless with laughter.

"Maybe the three of you should go on the road with that act," Brett interrupted. "It doesn't seem like you're very interested in law enforcement."

The occupants of the room stared up in shocked silence. Cora and Pamela carefully and quietly inched around him to get back to the bullpen. Carl and Larry collided as they each ran in opposite directions. Simultaneously they mumbled, "Sorry Chief," and squeezed out the door next. Lisa was frozen in place with a shamed look on her face.

"I'm more disappointed in you then anyone else," Brett told her. "I remember when you first moved here from Atlanta. You were in Nina's seventh grade class. Was there a single day you didn't get picked on and bullied? I remember having to drive you back and forth to school the whole first semester. We talked about my criminology classes. I'd like to think that's what got you into this job. You were lucky Nina wanted to be your friend. Ginny hasn't found anyone who's that good-hearted yet. I was hoping it would be you she could turn to when she needed a friend outside of the family. I guess I was wrong."

Tears welled up in Lisa's eyes. "Oh Chief, I'm so sorry."

Brett wasn't in the mood to let her off the hook yet. He turned and left the room without a word. He kept walking past his other deputies and out the front doors.

****

The air conditioner was being replaced outside the open windows of Ginny's classroom. There was no breeze so the only thing coming in was the loud banging and occasional cursing from the workers. It was past noon, the hottest time of the day, and Ginny faced the most difficult class so far. Thankfully it was her final one of the day and she could spend the last hour on paperwork.

But for now, she had finally come face to face with the Harvey boys. They were sitting together at the back of the room entertaining the other students with rude noises and unsavory comments.

Fifteen-year-old Cole had a lean build and a bad complexion. His brown stringy hair fell to the shoulders of his faded camo T-shirt. His old army issue fatigue pants hung loosely over dirty sneakers. The book she'd assigned to him had been tossed on the floor and kicked under his chair.

Kyle was a year older, but had failed a grade in elementary school. No hair showed from under his straw cowboy hat, but the peach fuzz on his chin was the same medium brown as his brother's hair. He wore a plaid cotton shirt, open over his flat, hairless chest, and worn-out jeans with work boots. Ginny suspected his book was the source of the spit wads on her blackboard.

These were the two boys she'd defended to Brett.

"For your first assignment, I'd like you to write a five-hundred word essay about yourselves so I can get to know you better and see what you've learned so far. It'll be due on Monday."

"I'd rather write a story about a schoolteacher who gets taken by an Indian chief," Kyle yelled out. "I'll call it 'Big Chief Bangs Blondie.'"

The girls gasped and the other boys snickered.

"You better turn that around, bro," Cole put in. "From what I hear, the women do *all* the work in the teepee."

Kyle looked at Ginny with a serious expression. "Is that right, Ms. Silverfeather? Does the chief make you ride him like a pony?"

The whole class chuckled and mumbled.

"That's enough, you two," Ginny warned.

"I wanna know if he uses those handcuffs when he beds ya," Cole added.

Kyle laughed. "Only after she's been in a bar brawl, right Ms. Silverfeather? I bet that gets a big man like the chief all excited. Old Ms. Simmons says you already had your shirt half tore off when you come out of Hooligan's yesterday. You musta been getting ready for him."

"Stop this right now," Ginny said sternly.

Cole broke in again. "I hear the chief was too busy and sent his old grandpa to do the job."

Everyone laughed, including the workers outside.

"So, which one was with your dad when he had the cuffs on?" another scruffy boy named Horace Newman asked.

Both Harvey boys dove at Horace and within seconds the entire room was in bedlam.

Brett stood outside the door of the old mobile unit. It was bad enough when his men were hiding in a back room gossiping and making fun at his wife's expense. Now the kids at school were being openly disrespectful. He'd be surprised if she lasted the whole year.

He opened the door and shouted, "Break it up!"

Kyle stood up and grinned with his hat askew. "Well if it ain't Cochise hisself. Have you come to take scalps, Chief?"

Cole stood up next. "Circle the wagons and hide the women, guys, looks like the chief is on the warpath."

Brett walked in and took both Harvey boys by their collars. "You're coming with me."

Ginny rushed toward them. "You can't just walk in here and take my students away."

Brett gave her an evil look. "Watch me."

After the Harvey boys had been hauled away, the other students slowly began picking up books, papers and overturned chairs. They mumbled among themselves and no one made eye contact with Ginny. She certainly knew what the conversations would be around their dinner tables tonight. They'd tell their parents the new teacher had lost control and had two students arrested. Maybe Jake would like an interview for the paper. She proceeded to calmly write out the format for their essays on the blackboard and prayed for the class to end quickly.

After the class had been dismissed, Ginny slumped back in her chair and closed her eyes. A moment later the door clicked open. She reluctantly opened her eyes. Mrs. Dagget walked in looking as smug as ever.

"I thought you'd want to know the Harvey boys have been suspended from school for the rest of the week. I'm sure their educations will benefit greatly by that." She started to turn away and then changed her mind. "Mrs. Silverfeather, do you create this much trouble everywhere you go?"

It seemed she did, but Ginny wouldn't give her enemy the satisfaction of admitting it. Instead she simply stared back until Henrietta left the classroom. Ginny finished her first official day as a schoolteacher by crying her eyes out at her desk.

****

Brett had had plenty of time to finish his paperwork. The office had been quiet. He hadn't seen anyone from the night shift for the rest of the day and the day shift people were avoiding him. He'd seen them whispering among themselves a few times, but their expressions were serious. Occasionally, they'd glance his way.

On the way out, Brett stopped by Cora's desk. "Could you please call my wife and let her know I won't be able to make it home for dinner tonight?"

"Of course," Cora responded.

"Would you also tell her she shouldn't wait up for me? I have a few things to take care of."

"Chief." Cora looked up with a pained expression. "I hope we haven't caused a problem at your house. I'm sure your wife is a very sweet person."

"Yes, she is," Brett said, "and I can't think of a single reason why she should be. I'm very disappointed with the reception she's had since she got here. I can't imagine what she must think of this town. You should all be less concerned with what goes on in my house and more concerned with your jobs."

Brett took off his arm sling and threw it in the trash bin. It had become an annoyance. He grabbed the keys to his county SUV and drove to the diner.

The Blue Bird Diner was slow on Tuesday nights, but even more so after a long holiday weekend. There were only about a dozen people inside. Brett didn't feel up to socializing anyway. Usually he would have sat at the counter, but tonight he walked straight to a booth at the back. He ordered a hamburger and a cup of coffee. He wasn't really hungry, but he needed a reason to be there. What he did want was a little time to himself to think.

He'd really stepped on Ginny's toes by taking the Harvey boys out of her classroom the way he had. She was right. It hadn't been his place. She needed to assert her authority over her students and he'd screwed that up on her very first day. He didn't know why he'd done it. It just rubbed his last nerve to hear those boys talking to her the way they had.

After Clive had talked to the boys, Brett had

driven them home. It set him back a little when Kyle asked him to drop them off out by the road. He'd intended to speak to their mother, but Kyle had told him she wouldn't want him in their house. She was mad because her husband was still in jail.

There were some things Brett just couldn't figure out. He'd arrested the man who'd held Mrs. Harvey at gunpoint, the same man who put a nasty bruise on her jaw, and she was mad at him for it.

Would he ever understand women? He'd done the best he could for her and Ginny, but he was the one in the doghouse with both of them.

Poppy sat across from him with a cup of coffee in his hand. "What are you doing here, Little Chief? You've got a wife to cook for you now."

Brett was never surprised by Poppy's unexpected appearances. The man had a tendency to pop up everywhere. Poppy was the only person who still called him Little Chief, and the only one who could still get away with it.

"Two reasons," Brett answered. "The first being, Ginny hasn't really caught on to cooking yet so she may accidentally poison me. The second is, I made an ass of myself with her today and so she may poison me on purpose."

"It's hard to settle into a new marriage under normal circumstances," Poppy said. "The two of you haven't found your way to each other yet. It'll take time, have patience."

"I'm not sure that'll ever happen, Poppy. Maybe you were wrong about her. Maybe she's not my dove after all. Maybe your vision was just brought on by the greasy chili you eat at Hooligan's every day. What do you suppose that stuff is doing to your stomach?"

"Don't insult Sean's chili. It's the only pleasure I have left. Besides that, I won't be using this stomach much longer. Before I die I want a great-grandson."

Brett rolled his eyes. "Don't pull the one-foot-in-the-grave routine with me, old man. You're as healthy as a horse. And you already have three great-grandsons and two great-granddaughters just from our part of the family. Did you forget that? I could call Jake and Julie and let them remind you." Brett raised his cell phone and wiggled it in front of Poppy.

Poppy slumped back indignantly. "Of course I didn't forget. I love all those kids, but this is different. You'll be the leader of our band some day. You'll need a son to take over for you when the time comes."

"A son with Ginny would be half white. Or maybe there would be only daughters." Brett turned his coffee cup in a circle on the table. "Ginny would be a terrific mother. But the way things are going so far, there may not be any children, not with me anyway."

"Are you saying your wife is refusing you?" Poppy asked with astonishment. "Silverfeather blood runs hot in your veins. I don't believe this has ever happened before."

"Chill out, Poppy," Brett replied. "To be honest, we just haven't gotten that far yet. Let's not forget that I only met the woman eight days ago, and then I got shot the day after I married her."

Brett felt his seat lift when the person on the other side of the divider stood up. He glanced over the top and looking back at him was Orville Dagget. Opposite from Poppy, Henrietta stood. They were both smiling. Brett could have cut out his own tongue at that moment. There was no doubt they'd heard every word he and Poppy had spoken.

"Ready for the big rally this weekend, Chief?" Dagget asked.

Brett had almost forgotten he and Dagget were both giving campaign speeches at the Heritage Day

Festival on Saturday. He'd rather take a sharp stick in his side than have to give another speech, but he'd do anything to keep his job...and to keep Dagget from getting it.

"I guess I'm as ready as I'll ever be, Dagget."

"Good, good." Dagget grinned. "I hope you'll be bringing the wife with you. I just may have some surprises for you. I'd hate for her to miss it."

"She'll be there," Brett answered coolly. "I wouldn't think of going without her."

"Of course you wouldn't," Henrietta smirked, "but where is Mrs. Silverfeather now?"

"She stayed at home to relax and plan for her class tomorrow."

Henrietta passed her husband a knowing glace. "That's wonderful. I know she needs plenty of time to try to put something constructive together. The poor thing seems to be struggling. Some of us don't have a natural ability for the career paths we choose."

The Daggets gave Brett and Poppy a pleasant good-bye and walked to the cash register with their check.

"I really hate that guy," Brett said as he watched Dagget pay his bill.

Chapter Eleven

After coming home late on Tuesday night, something had changed in Brett. He still seemed distant to Ginny, but not in an angry way. He actually seemed contemplative.

Brett took over the care of the animals and spent more time with the horses than he had in the first week. He was finally able to dress himself, although Ginny still helped with his bandages. He didn't complain about her cooking, even though she still made mistakes. Every evening at dinner he politely asked about her day. He worked at his computer or read before he went to bed.

Sometimes she would look up from grading papers and find him watching her. He would play it off by asking if she wanted something from the kitchen or if she had enough light to work by. There was never any mention of the incident at Hooligan's or in her classroom. There was also no repeat of the jokes and teasing he had started before then. It seemed as though Brett was in deep thought at all times and couldn't be disturbed. Yes, contemplative was a good word for the way he was acting now. It wasn't unpleasant, but it wasn't pleasurable either. They seemed like two strangers sharing a house, which Ginny had to remind herself, they were.

Without the Harvey boys in class, things settled down at school as well. The little wrinkles in her job were ironing themselves out and Ginny felt good about the results. She was really getting a chance to stretch her wings as a teacher.

Ginny had chosen a different book for each of

her classes to analyze and discuss. The homework assignment each night was a newspaper type review of the chapter they would cover in class the next day. Once she had surprised them by asking them to write a faux interview with one of the characters in their book.

In the hallway on Friday, she overheard some of her students talking about what they were each reading. One girl commented that Ms. Silverfeather's classroom was more like a book club than actual school. They seemed to be satisfied with the format, which satisfied her as well.

Ginny ate lunch in the teacher's lounge and had begun to make a few friends among the other teachers. The male teachers were extremely attentive and helpful. The female teachers were full of questions about what it was like to live with the chief. She just smiled and told them what a wonderful man he was to put up with her domestic challenges. When they mentioned his occasional surliness she pretended she hadn't noticed anything of the kind. They'd walk away wondering what secrets she kept hidden. She often wished she did have a secret or two to hide about Brett. She certainly wouldn't tell the kind of tales about him that Diana had, even if she could.

Now the week was over, it was Saturday, and she had a new milestone to pass. This was the first time she would actually go out in public as Brett's wife. She'd be standing beside him as he gave his campaign speech for re-election. What did a person wear for something like that?

****

"I'll meet you at the car," Brett called through her closed bedroom door. "I've got to load up a few boxes of bumper stickers and campaign pins for my booth."

Brett crossed the front porch and down the steps

where he'd parked. It was a good day for an outing. The temperature wasn't expected to climb over the high seventies and a nice breeze made wearing his uniform a little more bearable.

He lifted the small boxes, two at a time, into the back of his SUV. It barely caused a twinge in his shoulder now. Not only was he a fast healer, but Ginny had been fastidious about taking care of his wound.

That was a benefit to being married he hadn't considered. Maybe someday coming home to a home-cooked meal would be a benefit as well. Today, he was looking forward to finding a hotdog vender. Last night's meatloaf had kept him up half the night.

He did have to admit, though, Ginny had become a pleasant companion.

Ginny bounced out of the house wearing a dress he hadn't seen before, but he wasn't likely to forget. It was a simple navy blue sundress covered in tiny white polka dots. It had a full skirt that nearly touched her knees, but the top was formfitting and showed just enough cleavage to make him wish for more. She wore white sandals and a thin white sweater over her shoulders. The sides of her hair were pulled back by a headband, leaving the long column of her neck exposed. He wanted to kiss his way down her neck and right into the top of that dress. He was suddenly as horny as a sixteen-year-old with his first Playboy opened to the centerfold.

Ginny smiled up at him. "Can I turn on the lights and siren?"

"Absolutely."

****

For the sake of decorum, Ginny didn't turn on the lights and siren. She was excruciatingly aware that all eyes would be on her and Brett today. The rally for the candidates could possibly make or break his career. If she was to be a factor in anyone's decision, she wanted to be a positive one.

They parked at the courthouse and walked through town. They were greeted by cordial smiles and nods as they admired the arts and crafts displayed along the sidewalk. He bought Ginny a pair of earrings from the booth outside Mandy's store. They were silver and in the shape of tiny feathers. Then he bought them each a strawberry ice cream cone outside the diner. He stopped to speak to several people along the way, but he held her hand the entire time. Ginny wished the gesture of affection wasn't just for show. She wished they could be like this every day.

Brett still held her hand as he talked to Clive Winters about the school's first football game of the season and who this year's star players would be. He still held on to her as they spoke to Lisa Jackson and Sean from Hooligans Bar and Grill. Ginny hadn't realized Sean was Lisa's father.

Brett only let go of her hand when he greeted his mother with a hug, but immediately placed his arm around Ginny's shoulders.

The spell was broken when his deputy, Larry Graham, called from across the street. "Chief, they need you over at the bandstand. They want to have the coin toss."

Ginny gazed up at Brett and cocked her head. "The coin toss?"

"They toss a coin to decide which candidate gets to speak first." Brett checked the display on his cell phone. "The election rally is supposed to start in fifteen minutes. I guess I'd better get over there."

They both threw what remained of their ice cream cones in a trash bin.

Worry lines formed between Ginny's eyes. "You have to give your speech now? I hope you're not as nervous as I am."

Brett used his thumb to wipe a dab of ice cream

from the center of her bottom lip and smiled. "It'll be all right. I'll be right there next to you the whole time.

When they reached the bandstand the Daggets were already there. The other couple stood looking out over the crowd as if they were addressing the media in the rose garden of the White House. Ginny finally had her first look at her husband's opposition. Seeing Henrietta and Orville Dagget together made her want to giggle. An old nursery rhyme began playing in her head, "Jack Sprat could eat no fat, and his wife could eat no lean." Orville Dagget was as thin as his wife was round. He was also more than a foot taller than Henrietta.

Henrietta noticed Brett and Ginny approaching. She nudged her husband and stood on her toes to whisper something near his ear. When he looked down at her, she nodded their way. Ginny was used to the snarky smile Henrietta always gave her, but Orville's self-satisfied smirk made her skin crawl.

Orville Dagget was a perfect fit for the part of Ichabod Crane in The Legend of Sleepy Hollow. Ginny guessed his age to be close to sixty. His hair was a drab brown and thinning. His eyes were small, sunken, and dark. His nose was like the beak of a crow. He had virtually no lips around a smile that revealed small, dark teeth. The starched white collar of his dress shirt hung loosely around a long neck with a protruding adam's apple. There was something sinister looking about him. Perhaps it was just that she'd always been scared by the story of Sleepy Hollow.

She tried to look past the conservative blue suit and prep school striped tie to imagine him wearing the green uniform that Brett wore so well. The image just wouldn't come together for her.

"Shall we get started, Silverfeather?" Orville Dagget said. "I'm feeling lucky today. I think I'll call heads."

Mayor Tom Brewster flipped a silver dollar into the air and caught it on the way down. He slapped it onto the back of his hand and then pulled his other hand back to reveal the coin. "Heads it is," the mayor announced.

Brett led Ginny to their chairs on the right side of the bandstand while Henrietta sat alone in one of the two chairs on the left. The mayor and city councilmen sat in the center behind the podium.

"Is it bad for you that he gets to go first?" Ginny whispered to Brett.

"No, I'd prefer to go last," Brett explained. "This way I can address any issues that may come as a surprise."

Orville reached into the inside pocket of his jacket for a small stack of index cards.

"Did you make notes to work from?" Ginny asked, again whispering.

"Nope, don't need any. I've known most of these people my whole life. I know how to talk to them."

Instead of notes, Brett pulled his leather bound notepad and pen from his breast pocket and crossed one leg over the other to use as a makeshift desk.

"Let the good times roll," Brett whispered.

"Ladies and gentlemen of Three Trees, my name is Orville Dagget, your next sheriff. Let me begin by welcoming our newest resident and schoolteacher, Mrs. Virginia Silverfeather, wife of the current and soon former sheriff."

When he extended his arm in Ginny's direction the crowd clapped politely. Ginny hadn't expected to be pointed out and didn't appreciate his arrogance. She waved with a weak smile toward the audience.

"I know many of you have been concerned about the sheriff's lack of family responsibility and ties to the community, especially after he was jilted by his longtime girlfriend only weeks before their marriage.

As you can see he's found a suitable replacement."

Dagget paused.

"At least we'd like to assume she'd be suitable. We only met Mrs. Silverfeather less than two weeks ago. That was the night she drove her car into a canal outside of town. Thankfully there were no other cars involved. As a matter of fact, there was no evidence as to what caused the accident. However, she was rescued and whisked to the clinic immediately.

"In my term as sheriff I will require drug and alcohol testing at such accident sights, not that I believe our new schoolteacher was under the influence, of course."

The crowd began to whisper. Dagget waited for their attention to refocus on him.

"But then, some of us may remember that only three days later, Mrs. Silverfeather was brought into her husband's office in handcuffs. Was it just another driving incident or something more? When she was stopped for speeding by the Georgia Highway Patrol, they found a concealed weapon in Mrs. Silverfeather's possession. This time, though, the patrolman handed her over to the good sheriff and all was forgotten, no report was ever filed. It seems our sheriff has made the right kind of friends."

The crowd shifted uncomfortably, their smiles gone. All the times Brett warned her that her actions could compromise his position were coming back to haunt Ginny. If he lost the election because of her she wouldn't be able to live with herself.

"This is not to say that our jails stay empty," Dagget continued. "Only five days later three tourists visiting our sleepy little town were arrested after a brawl in Hooligan's bar. One of the gentlemen suffered abrasions and contusions to his face during his arrest. A lady lost her front tooth.

The second man came out barely better than his friends. Did I mention Mrs. Silverfeather was also involved in that fight...in a bar...in the middle of the day? Not only was she involved, but so were Sheriff Silverfeather's grandfather and the owner of the establishment. All three were released at the scene. I'm glad to see Mrs. Silverfeather is also making friends."

This time the crowd stood in shocked silence, waiting.

"Now I'm not saying any of this makes Mrs. Silverfeather a bad teacher for your children. She seems to be quite popular among most of her students. She must have gained their respect the first day. It was the day when her husband, the sheriff, dropped by her classroom to find she'd lost control of her class. He removed two boys from the room and escorted them to the principal's office where they were suspended for the rest of their first week of school."

The crowd looked around and nodded to each other, having already heard the story.

"These were two very troubled students I feel needed a different kind of attention. Only days before they had seen their own father arrested by our sheriff's deputies.

"As I hear the story, the sheriff had control of the situation and had even invited the man to join him for breakfast. When the man approached, he was drawn on by a deputy. The man was startled and in fear for his life. His gun discharged hitting the sheriff in the shoulder. Does anyone truly believe a man would take aim at the person he was intending to join for breakfast only seconds earlier? Did the sheriff really have control of the situation, or even his own deputies? I'd like to ask you how two impressionable young boys are supposed to behave after witnessing such a thing outside of their own home."

Ginny couldn't look out into the crowd, but she did glance over to see Brett's fingers had tightened around his pen to the point of turning his knuckles white. She couldn't read the scribble on his pad but she could see that the impression of his pen had gone deeper. She closed her eyes when Dagget continued.

"Now let's not forget folks, this all happened on the heels of a new marriage. We all know how stressful that can be. Just the other night Sheriff Silverfeather was at the diner complaining about his wife's lack of domestic skills. It seems he was in search of a decent meal."

That comment was answered by a twitter of laughter among the crowd.

"As a matter of fact, food wasn't the only thing he mentioned was missing from their marriage. This isn't the time or place to discuss such personal matters, but we all know there are certain things that are essential in making a marriage work, a certain amount of, shall we say, closeness that's required."

Ginny was startled into looking up at her husband. His eyes were full of regret before he returned them to his lap.

"They do make an attractive couple as we can all finally see. Even though the Silverfeather's are known to be a close-knit clan, I believe this is the first time I've seen the newlyweds out together. But perhaps I'm wrong. Has anyone else ever seen them together? That is, when Mrs. Silverfeather wasn't in handcuffs?"

The whispering in the crowd grew a little louder as people conferred with each other.

"Well, I'm sure we'll all get to know Mrs. Silverfeather in time. The sheriff can get to know her right along with the rest of us."

Dagget paused.

"It seems the sheriff was so desperate to replace his runaway bride, he married a woman he'd never laid eyes on until she arrived in town less than two weeks ago."

He turned to look at Brett and Ginny as the crowd stood silent again. "My wife and I would like to wish you both all the luck we've had over the twenty-five years we've been together. There's nothing like the security that comes from a stable and loving home life."

The whispers far outweighed the applause as Orville Dagget took his seat, but he seemed satisfied.

Brett returned the pad and pen he'd been using to his shirt pocket and stood. To Ginny's utter amazement, he reached for her hand and led her to the podium. He placed his arm around her waist and pulled her into his side.

"Hi everybody," he began, "as Mr. Dagget pointed out, I've been recently married. It's still hard to let go, and so I hope you won't mind if my new wife keeps me company up here."

Reluctant grins broke out among the crowd. Ginny smiled back nervously.

"I was a little surprised by the fact that my opponent chose to discuss my wife and marriage, in lieu of the usual campaign speech about issues. But you all know me. After all, I was born and raised right here in Three Trees. You know how I hate speeches. So, I feel like I can do no less than follow his lead.

"No, I don't intend to talk about Mrs. Dagget. What can I say that you don't already know? The Dagget's have made their presence known here since they moved from Ohio ten years ago. A lot of you have encountered Mrs. Dagget at the school, when your children have stepped out of line. I'm sure you all recall those experiences. And many of us have seen Mr. Dagget in the courtroom as a defense attorney. I know I'll never forget being on the witness stand and facing his questions when he was defending someone I'd had to arrest."

He let the connotation of the last statement settle in.

"The subject today, however, seems to be my marriage and that's a subject I could talk about all day, but I promise to let you off with a shorter summary."

The crowd seemed to be a little more relaxed now and moved forward slightly.

"What Mr. Dagget said is true, folks. I met my wife online. As you know, I'd been single for a year. I was on the internet one night and ran across an ad about a young woman who was looking for a teaching position. I knew we were in need of a teacher here and e-mailed her to ask for her resume. My intention was to hand it over to the school board and let them take it from there, and I did. But then Ginny and I started a dialogue and as they say, the rest is history.

"Ginny gave up her home and friends in Michigan to come here and be my wife. Her beauty, charm, and boundless sense of humor were a complete surprise to me. My stubbornness and bluster were unfortunately a surprise to her. So I'll admit, it hasn't been easy, but she's making a difference in me. I think she'll make a difference in a lot of us.

"I've never known anyone who loved children and teaching the way she does. I figure I'll have the happiest, smartest kids in town someday. And no, there isn't anything to announce yet, but we're working on it. With luck, we'll have more to say on the subject within the next year."

The whispers took on a happier tone as people

smiled at each other.

"I'll admit there've been a few mishaps, like the accident that happened outside of town when a deer ran out in front of Ginny's car. That's happened to a few of us, so you can just imagine how frightening it was for a woman that had never driven outside the city at night.

"Then there was the misunderstanding of the concealed weapon that turned out to be an authentic American Indian war knife. If any of you guys want to come by and see it, I keep it on my mantel at home. It was my wedding gift from Ginny and I have to admit, I'm pretty darned proud of it.

"Unfortunately, the worse thing that's happened since Ginny arrived was the assault on her by the hunters who were drinking at Hooligan's, when she went in to meet my grandfather for lunch. I'd like to publicly thank Poppy and Sean for keeping her safe until I could get there. I wouldn't want her or anyone else here to feel they aren't safe anywhere in Three Trees. I do my best, but sometimes we have to look out for each other, and there's no one I'd rather count on than all of you."

The crowd looked around nodding proudly at each other.

"But then Ginny might say the worst thing that's happened was spending the day after our wedding in the hospital. The last thing a new bride needs to hear is that her husband's been shot. I guess that brings me to the insinuation that Mr. Dagget found necessary to make about my love life. I wasn't in good shape for a while there. I want to apologize to my wife for having mentioned something so personal where it could be overheard."

The crowd looked at Dagget with contempt.

"I also have to admit," Brett continued, "we have had a few mishaps at home, but only in the kitchen. I look at it this way. A woman can't be expected to have brains, beauty and also the talents of Julia Child. If there's one I'd have to give up, well, I don't mind going out to eat now and then. Also, I'd just like to add that she can ride as well as I can and camping under the stars doesn't bother her a bit. Now that's my kind of woman."

Brett looked down at her with tenderness.

"The best thing I can share with you about Ginny is that she's determined. She's finding more innovative methods of teaching to her students. She's anxious to become a part of our community and she's doing her best to civilize me. And don't think she can't do it, she's already turning my dog, Bear, into a sissy."

He got a genuine laugh that time.

"In conclusion," Brett said, "I want you all to know I'm a proud man. I'm proud of my lovely wife, my supportive family, and I'm proud of my hometown. I intend to keep it a safe place for all of us to raise our children."

The crowd let out hoots and hollers as he lifted Ginny against his chest and kissed her in front of the whole town.

Secretly, they were each wishing all he'd said was true.

126

Chapter Twelve

On Sunday morning, Ginny went into the kitchen to find a very attractive derriere poking out from behind the refrigerator door.

"How can you even think about food after last night?" she asked. "I don't think I'll ever be hungry again."

After returning from the Heritage Day festivities, several of the ladies from town had dropped by with covered dishes and decadent desserts. Each had attached a recipe card to their contribution.

Brett looked at her over the top of the refrigerator door. "I'm still up to my eyeballs with Mrs. Bennett's swamp cabbage casserole. However, it seemed better last night than it does this morning. Now, I'm just trying to get to the milk before I die."

Ginny didn't know what swamp cabbage was, but she'd found out she liked it. For that reason, she'd been reluctant to ask where it came from.

"I've got what you need right here," she said with a sexy smile.

Brett's eyebrows rose with interest and then relaxed with a grin when Ginny pulled a roll of antacids from the pocket of her pajama pants.

"You're a Goddess," he claimed as he chewed one of the tablets.

Since the election rally the day before, Ginny and Brett both understood they needed to pose as a loving couple for their friends and neighbors. At home, however, Ginny had moved up in status from unwanted houseguest to companionable roommate.

Occasionally she thought she saw a look of desire in Brett's eyes, but then he'd turn away. She decided it was just the product of her own wishful thinking.

She'd never truly desired a man before. The men in her life had always been the first to make a move. Physical intimacy had merely been a requirement for a personal relationship, an unavoidable requirement she'd simply tolerated. Now she was living with a man, for the first time in her life, and he was totally hands-off. Besides a couple of kisses that had nearly made her insides melt, he hadn't touched her. The irony there was that she wanted him so much it made her crazy. He was the reluctant one in this relationship, which was destroying her self-confidence. One name kept nagging the back of her mind, Diana. Was he really over her?

"I have to go into the office this morning to finish some paperwork." Brett pulled the keys from his pocket and picked up his hat. "Barring disaster, I should be home early. Is there anything you'd like to do tonight?"

Ginny didn't dare answer the question honestly. "I've got everything ready for school tomorrow and we certainly don't need to worry about food for the next month. We can just relax and play it by ear."

"Sounds good." Brett impulsively leaned over and kissed her cheek before he jogged out the back door and down the steps to his car. Ginny stared after him with her fingertips lightly touching where his lips had been.

****

It was past one o'clock when Brett finally cleared his desk. He would have been finished before noon, if he hadn't had every woman in town come by to let him know he'd won their vote with the speech he'd given at the rally. Some of them had even dragged their husbands along.

The table in the corner of the outer office was

covered with cookies and cupcakes. Brett smiled. If he got any more lovable he'd have to buy larger clothes.

Another tap sounded on the door. Brett stood and walked around his desk when his aunt, Marsha, entered.

Marsha stood on tiptoe and stretched to reach Brett's cheek for a kiss. "I was out doing a little shopping and decided to stop by when I saw your car."

"I'm glad you did," Brett said, as he directed her to a chair in front of his desk. He took the chair beside her rather than sitting with the desk between them. "How's everything at home?"

"Good," she answered, "and I'm glad to see things are going so well for you and Ginny. I have to admit, I had my doubts."

"We're getting to know each other."

"I hope so. I've been a little curious about her."

"Why is that?" Brett asked.

"Well," Marsha hesitated, "it's probably none of my business. It's just that I've been looking over her records. Has she ever said anything to you about her family or her home life growing up?"

Brett thought back on the night after their wedding when they'd slept outdoors. "Ginny mentioned that her father had left when she was young. I think she was an only child. She also mentioned she'd been in a few foster homes."

Marsha looked exasperated. "Is that it? Did you ask if she'd ever heard from her father after he'd left? Did you ask what happened to her mother? Did you ask why she'd gone into the system?"

Brett hoped he didn't look as embarrassed as he felt. He made an effort to keep his voice pleasant. "I figured she'd tell me when she was ready. In my line of work you see a lot of screwed up families. Why are you asking about all this anyway?"

Marsha opened a folder that she had carried in her large purse. "Ginny's high school records were in the package that arrived from her college. It was probably just a mix-up. They don't usually send them. I was a little disturbed by what I found though." She shifted uncomfortably in her chair. "I wouldn't normally say anything, except she's your wife and my niece. They don't look good, Brett."

"So she wasn't a great student in high school. She was a teenager. She seemed to make up for it in college."

"No, she was an excellent student all the way through, which is amazing." Marsha's continued hesitance worried Brett. He waited silently for her to continue, which she did. "Twice in the first semester of ninth grade she was absent from school for hospital stays. She must have been thirteen or fourteen then. Do you know if she has any health issues?"

Brett frowned. "She doesn't seem to. I've never thought to ask. It could have just been something simple though, tonsils, pneumonia, any number of things."

"Except she was put in foster care after the second time," Marsha said. "Her records were signed by five different foster parents between then and the end of her junior year. She changed schools each time, but she always stayed in Saginaw County. She'd been emancipated by the time she started her senior year. She had just turned seventeen. As far as I can tell, she was on her own after that. She got through college on scholarships and grants. She's a very smart girl. But, her only emergency contact was a social worker from the child services department."

Brett was confused.

Why hadn't Ginny said anything to him about all this? Had he ever given her an opening to talk to him? Was this the secret he sometimes saw hidden behind sad eyes?

"I'd like the name of the social worker."

"I can give you that," Marsha drew a notepad out of her purse, "but don't you think you should talk to Ginny first."

After Marsha had gone, Brett paced his office. It was nearly impossible to get information on a Sunday. Not everyone had to work the way cops did. On impulse Brett called the Saginaw County Sheriff's Department.

After brief introductions he got right to the point. "I'd like you to send me any information on cases you've had for the last ten years in connection with a woman named Virginia Dearing. She would have been thirteen years old at the beginning of that time."

"Can you tell me what this is in reference to, Sheriff Silverfeather?" the woman who'd identified herself as Deputy Linden asked.

Brett didn't want to give the impression he was spying on his wife so he didn't mention he was married to Ginny. Instead he said, "She recently moved to my area and she's been having some trouble. We think it may involve someone from her past. I don't want to leave any stone unturned. How fast can you have something to me?"

"I'll put her information in our computer and send you what we have. I can e-mail you within twenty-four hours."

Brett gave the woman all the information he could on Ginny. He also gave her his personal e-mail address. He had a bad feeling about what would turn up and he didn't want to share it with anyone else in the department. He followed by leaving a message for the caseworker whose name Marsha had given him as Barbara Henson.

Upon returning home, Brett found the house quiet and empty. He'd seen Ginny's car in the drive and decided she must be busy outside. He changed into a T-shirt and jeans to join her, and then checked the barn. Bear and Cin were also missing. He could only think of one place Ginny knew of to go on the property. As he saddled Havoc, he reasoned it was as good a place as any for he and Ginny to have a long talk.

****

Ginny knew the warm summer days were numbered. Soon the trees would be changing color and shedding their leaves and there'd be a chill in the air. Probably not as early as in Michigan, but she wanted to enjoy the summer for as long as she could. Her favorite summer activity was a nice leisurely swim. Thankfully, the lake Brett had taken her to on their wedding night afforded plenty of privacy. She hadn't thought to bring a bathing suit when she'd left the house. She didn't feel there was anything to worry about, though. Brett never got out of the office before five and she knew Bear wouldn't tell.

When Ginny stood on a sandbar in the center of the lake the water reached a few inches above her waist. She flipped her hair back and rubbed the water from her eyes. Just as she opened her eyes she heard a familiar deep voice behind her.

"Public nudity is a serious crime in my town, Mrs. Silverfeather. You're under arrest. Come out with your hands up."

Ginny crossed her arms over her breasts and spun around. She found Brett kneeling at the water's edge smiling at her. Havoc was tied up next to Cin at the edge of the clearing. Bear was at Brett's side having his ears scratched...the traitor. He hadn't made a sound to warn her someone was approaching. Of course, he wouldn't have taken Brett as a threat, but still, he knew she was naked. Oh damn, so did Brett now. How much had he seen before he'd said anything.

Ginny dropped to her knees to hide herself and had to struggle to keep her face above water. She thought about her options. She didn't have a towel and she didn't have dry clothes. The thin white sundress she'd left on a bush was several yards away and would be transparent over her wet skin. She realized she only had one option. She'd stay in the water until he went away. As stubborn as he was, she expected to be the size and texture of a prune by then.

Brett looked around the clearing. His mind must have been going down the same path. "I'd say you've gotten yourself into a little bit of a pickle, Dove. What are you going to do now?"

"If you were a gentleman, you'd turn your back." As much as Ginny wanted to sound indignant, her voice wavered and her teeth chattered.

"Will it make you any less naked?"

"No."

Brett stood, still smiling, and drew his good arm out of his T-shirt. He pulled it over his head before sliding it off his injured shoulder. He left the shirt on a dry rock and backed a few feet away before turning around.

Ginny had already noticed the way his jeans rode an inch or two below the low waistband of his briefs. He had one of those half in half out type belly buttons and what was called a pleasure trail of thin black hair.

With his back turned and his feet planted several inches apart, his bottom was tight and round. The legs of his jeans fit snuggly over heavy muscles in his thighs. She wondered if the day would ever come, when she would be free to explore all the intriguing areas of his body. Then she remembered, once those jeans were off, he'd be no different than the other men she'd known - rough, selfish, and demanding. She'd freeze up like she always had and the spell would be broken. It was best not to indulge in a sport she had no talent for.

Brett shifted a little. "Are you decent yet?"

"I try to be."

"Well, skinny-dipping isn't the best way to prove..."

When Brett turned back to her, his heart nearly leapt out of his chest. His faded green T-shirt almost reached her knees, but it clung to her wet body like a second skin. He could see the rapid rise and fall of her chest and the flush in her cheeks. Her eyes had gone wide and dark with what he suspected was sexual awareness. How much was a man expected to endure?

In one step forward and the reach of his arm, she was pressed against his chest and his tongue was stroking hers. Her mouth was warm and damp and tasted like mint tea. She smelled clean, yet earthy at the same time. Her fingertips were kneading his shoulders hesitantly, but her belly rubbed restlessly against his aching erection.

Brett broke the kiss to whisper against her cheek. "I need to touch you, Dove, before I completely lose my mind."

Ginny took his hand from her waist and placed it over her breast. A moan escaped her when he tugged at the hard tip under his fingers. That one soft sound was all the invitation he needed to go further. In the next breath, Ginny was laying on her back in the deep grass with the shirt pushed up to her shoulders.

Brett made an exploration of her body with his lips, tongue, and even the edges of his teeth. Ginny couldn't hold still, she couldn't stay quiet. He worked his way from her breasts to her toes and then settled into the cradle of her body to drive her insane. Ginny felt a kind of tingling, pulse pounding ecstasy she'd never felt before.

When the waves of euphoria subsided she reached for the zipper of his jeans. Brett did the most difficult thing he'd ever had to do. He caught her hand and pulled it away. He brought it up to place a kiss on her palm.

"I made you a solemn promise," Brett said with a tense voice. "If this goes any farther, I'll lose control. My word is my honor."

Ginny couldn't comprehend his meaning. He'd given her pleasure. He'd given her more than any other man ever had. Yet he didn't take anything for himself. It was evident by the bulge straining against his zipper and the look in his eyes he wanted more.

Just then his cell phone rang. Before answering it, Brett pulled the T-shirt back down over her body. He paused for a few seconds when he reached the apex of her thighs.

After she was covered, Brett stood and walked back to the edge of the water. His mind was in such a state of confusion he had to have Cora Marshall repeat the message she'd called with.

Although the conversation was short, Ginny was able to finish dressing behind a large bush. "Is everything all right?" Ginny asked from behind him.

"It's the Harvey boys again," Brett said, not turning around. "They were caught burglarizing a house. They'll have to go in front of a judge in the morning. I want to be there."

"Of course you do. I'll have classes, but I hope you'll call me as soon as it's over."

Brett still couldn't make himself look at Ginny. "Sure."

"Is anything else wrong?"

Brett brushed past her on his way to the horses. "I need to ride for a while, clear my head, you know. I may be out for a while."

Brett rode out at a loping dash. What had happened? Did he already regret what he'd done? That one name skittered across her mind again, Diana. Brett must have found his wife to be a poor replacement.

****

Brett thought about the report that would come in his e-mail the next day. He wasn't sure if he was ready to read what it said. After seeing the small tattoo inside the top of Ginny's thigh, he wasn't sure he could handle it.

He tried to recall all she'd said by the fire on their wedding night and compared the information to what Marsha had told him.

She'd been ten years old when her father left. She'd been fourteen when she'd gone into the system. What had happened in between? Then he remembered her exact words, "My mother had a string of crappy boyfriends." Was that what this CJ was? How many like him had been on her mother's string of crappy boyfriends?

Brett picked up a fallen tree limb and beat it against the tree's trunk until it had smashed into pieces. The violent act didn't help the thunderstorm inside his brain. Why hadn't he paid more attention? He was a cop. It was those instincts he'd picked up as a cop, which had caused him to look more closely at the tattoo than someone else might have.

He knew what the tear on that little red cherry signified. At first, he hadn't thought much of it. Maybe it was an impulsive act she'd had in college to mark her first time. But on closer inspection, he saw that the person who had marked her delicate skin had been conceited enough to initial his work. He'd even dated it with the year. The tattoo was ten years old. For God's sake, Ginny was only twenty-three now.

He thought about his own actions today and was

ashamed he'd pushed her so far the first time he'd gotten the chance. After what happened today, she must think he was no better than the man with the initials CJ.

If he ever found that man, he'd kill him.

Chapter Thirteen

Brett settled in behind his desk at six o'clock Monday morning. He powered on his computer and waited for it to boot up. Black coffee churned in his stomach like boiling acid. His stomach was rebelling against his brain's decision not to accept food. Brett wasn't sure which side of the battle he was on. He decided to wait and see how he felt after checking his e-mail.

While waiting, he thought about Ginny and the afternoon before. Their time together had started out so perfect. Watching her in the water had been like catching a glimpse of a fairy at play. Her sensual response to his kisses had been the most extraordinary event of his life. His memories of Diana certainly paled in comparison.

Ginny hadn't required cuddling or long conversation. She didn't need to ask about his feelings or talk about the future. She simply enjoyed the moment as much as he did. That is, as much as he could before seeing her damned tattoo. And then, like an ass, he'd run away and left her there.

Brett realized that he was staring at his desktop icons. He double clicked on the big blue E. When his personal internet home page appeared there was a star beside the envelope to let him know he had mail.

The size of the e-mail from the Saginaw County Sheriff's Office was larger than he'd expected. He glanced over the entries as soon as the document opened. Several cases were listed for several different people. The one thing they all had in common was Ginny.

Her mother was listed as Joyce Dearing, no middle name. He wondered if Ginny had a middle name. It was something a husband should know.

Joyce Dearing had been in a lot of trouble; public drunkenness, prostitution, assault, drug possession, all more than once. How was a woman like her allowed to raise a little girl in the first place?

What had her father been thinking to leave her alone with this monster? His name wasn't mentioned anywhere. He seemed to have disappeared into a puff of smoke. Brett wondered if the man had given a single thought to his child in the last thirteen years.

There'd been domestic disturbance calls to her house on three occasions. Each incident had involved a different man, her mother's boyfriends. Brett's skin crawled when he read the name on the first report, Charles Johnston.

The other two men were Harold Scofield and Lawrence Elliot. Had they also taken liberties with her? Had there been others?

Each report stated that the minor child in the home had injuries that she'd refused to explain. She'd probably been threatened to keep her mouth shut. Brett tried to picture Ginny as a thirteen-year-old girl. His stomach revolted even more. She was hardly bigger than a minute at twenty-three.

Reports had also been filed regarding the two hospital stays Marsha had mentioned. The first one was in the month of October. Ginny had suffered a concussion and a broken arm. She'd told them she fell from a ladder. The doctors had strongly suspected abuse due to the number of older injuries they'd found. Without her cooperation, the investigation had been dropped.

The second incident had been four months later

in February, the same month as her birthday. This time Ginny suffered multiple contusions, abrasions, and a spontaneous abortion.

Dear Lord. She'd been pregnant at the age of thirteen and miscarried at fourteen. He couldn't read anymore. Brett had just enough time to close the file before making a dash for the restroom to vomit.

After rinsing his mouth and washing his face, Brett looked at himself in the mirror. He'd thought like a cop for the last ten years, but he couldn't make his mind work that way now. He was a husband, no matter how the situation had come about. Ginny was his to protect now. She was his first priority. It was about damned time she was someone's first priority.

How did he move forward with her now that he had this information? His mind was blank. Should he insist she talk about her past? Did he want to make her relive it? No, not until she was ready. If she never decided to tell him, it would be her choice and he'd have to respect that.

That damned tattoo would always be a reminder for him of what had happened. How did he handle that? Brett closed his eyes and he could see her laughing. Dammit, she had more courage and character than most men he knew. He admired her even more for working to become an advocate for children now. She'd never allow a child in her care to fall between the cracks the way he suspected she had.

When he remembered he'd first thought of her as a spoiled brat, it made him feel ashamed. She deserved to be spoiled. She deserved a lot of good things. She certainly deserved better than him.

A tap sounded on the door, followed by Cora Marshall's voice. "Are you all right, Chief? Maybe I should have someone else go to the courthouse in your place."

"Shit." He hadn't meant to say that out loud. He'd forgotten about the Harvey boys.

****

Ginny was glad to be back in her classroom. The morning had been too quiet. Brett had left for work before she woke up. She'd lived alone for the last seven years, but in the last two weeks she'd gotten used to sharing breakfast with him. It was funny how an old habit could die so easily.

She didn't want to believe Brett was avoiding her. Instead, she'd convinced herself he had work to catch up on. Also, she knew he was worried about the Harvey boys. She was concerned as well.

She looked over at the two empty desks that would still be empty today in fifth period after Kyle and Cole's fate had been decided by a judge in juvenile court. She knew how tough it was to come from a dysfunctional family. Knowing they had clearly broken the law and may face jail time, she wondered if their future would be any better. Her heart ached for the boys. They'd never had the influence it took to become good, decent men.

Just then, three of the cheerleaders bounced through the door, Brenda Keller, Candy McDonald, and Tori Reagan. They were always the first students to arrive. They ran straight for Ginny's desk, books still in their arms and grins on their faces.

"I saw you at the rally on Saturday, Ms. Silverfeather." Brenda used the dramatic tone of voice only teenage girls could pull off. "Your husband is so hot and man, is he ever into you."

"Wow, that was some kiss," Tori broke in. "Does he kiss as good as he looks?"

"It was the most romantic thing I've ever seen," Candy sighed.

Ginny couldn't help grinning as her face grew warm. Was this the way her whole day would go?

And as it turned out, yes, all of her students had witnessed their kiss and they were talking about it.

****

Brett sat at the back of the small courtroom. He'd listened to two cases for shoplifting and one for trespassing. He felt the judge had been stern yet fair. All three kids had been sentenced to community service and released to their parents. The looks on their parents' faces indicated that their punishment wouldn't end with the judge's decision. But, it was Brett's guess the judge saved the biggest case for last. The boys hadn't had a chance to steal anything before they were caught, but B&E was a serious offense.

He'd almost not recognized Peggy Harvey when she'd entered the courtroom. She sat three rows ahead and to the left of him now. Mrs. Harvey was wearing an outdated floral dress that was a size or two smaller than it should have been and too fancy for the occasion. The red lipstick, rouge, and dark eyeliner on her face looked like it had been applied by a second grader. Her graying hair had been changed to a deep auburn that didn't go well with her complexion.

John Harvey was still in state lock-up, awaiting trial. He'd been charged with several offenses including assault on a police officer with a deadly weapon. Brett hoped he'd finally get the help he needed for his drinking problem.

He couldn't worry about them today, though. They were old enough to make their own decisions. The boys were all that mattered to him.

Cole and Kyle were smarter than they acted and were just reacting to their situation. What would life be like if you were young and didn't see anything brighter in your future than an old dirt farm? How did a kid have hope if they couldn't dream of succeeding at something special? Brett's mind turned to Ginny again. She'd figured it out. Maybe they would too.

A door opened at the front left side of the room. Cole and Kyle were both led in wearing handcuffs and shackles. Brett was shocked by their appearance. They'd only been in jail for the night, but they looked like they'd been in a dungeon for a month. The bluster and belligerence had been drained out of them. They walked slowly with their heads down and shoulders rounded. Their clothes were wrinkled and dirty. Both had purplish, half-moon shadows under their eyes. He'd just seen the boys six days ago. They appeared to have aged ten years since then.

Brett's attention turned to the judge. The heavyset middle-aged man leaded back in his chair looking at the boys with concern. He saw the judge glance over in Peggy Harvey's direction and Brett followed suit.

Mrs. Harvey scoffed at the boys and shifted in her chair, readjusting the purse on her lap. She looked put-upon and impatient.

The judge began, "Do you boys each understand the seriousness of the charge against you?"

Cole nodded as Kyle answered, "Yes sir, we do."

"What do you have to say for yourselves?" the judge asked.

"We didn't mean no harm, your honor," Kyle said. "We were lookin' for food and we thought nobody was home."

The judge spoke directly to Cole. "Have you given any thought to what juvenile detention might be like?"

Cole just nodded again.

"Speak up, boy." The judge spoke in a more gentle voice.

"They have warm beds and food there, sir." Cole's voice was thick with emotion. "We know it's tough, but it beats starvin'."

"How long has it been since you boys ate?"

"They gave us an egg sandwich and milk this mornin' for breakfast." Kyle was back to answering for them both. "For a few days before that, we ate what we could find."

Brett's stomach lurched with the image of the boys scavenging from garbage cans. He knew they didn't have any friends to count on besides each other. They'd always lived too far from town and been too tough.

The judge looked beyond the boys. "Mrs. Harvey, could you please stand and explain?"

Brett noticed that Mrs. Harvey primped a little as she rose to answer the judge. She seemed to be enjoying her new image.

"I can't take care of 'em anymore, Judge. They don't cause me nothin' but trouble. They got my dear husband arrested and then got throwed out of school. I put the two of 'em out of the house."

Other people in the room whispered and shifted uncomfortably. The judge tapped his gavel. "The way I heard it, ma'am, your husband was drunk and disorderly when he shot a law enforcement officer."

"I can handle my husband, Judge, but these boys went off and called the law. That's what started the whole mess." She gathered courage and added. "Now he's gonna be in jail for a long time. I just want to get on with my life. You just take those boys and lock 'em up too. I'm not takin' 'em with me."

The judge looked as flabbergasted as Brett felt. "Can I ask where you intend to go, Mrs. Harvey?"

Mrs. Harvey tried and failed to hold back a satisfied smile. "I'm movin' in with my sister in Savannah. I can git a job there and start a new life, just like in the movies."

The judge wore a look of disgust on his face. "Maybe that would be best for all concerned, Mrs.

Harvey. I'll have some papers for you to sign before you leave."

Mrs. Harvey looked happy and excited. "Yes sir, Judge. I can sign my name real good. I'd be happy to be done with it."

Brett looked back at Cole and Kyle. They didn't even look surprised, just resigned. His stomach tightened like a fist. How could he explain to Ginny that these boys had been thrown aside by their own mother, just like she had?

****

When Brett hadn't called to let Ginny know what the outcome had been in court, she could only imagine that the worst had happened. Cole and Kyle wouldn't be coming back. She felt she'd failed them. Even though their father had shot her husband, it had nothing to do with her relationship with the boys. She should have been able to make a connection with them that first day and kept control of her class. That's what a good teacher would have done. She promised herself she would make a better effort when they were released.

Who was she kidding; she couldn't even control what happened in her own marriage. She still couldn't figure Brett out. He yelled at her one day, and then appeared to be a loving husband the next. He looked at her with pure unadulterated lust one minute, and then couldn't face her at all.

She was having just as much trouble getting a handle on her own emotions lately. She'd never trusted a man since the day her father walked away, but she wanted to share everything with Brett. Brett, the most stubborn, bullheaded, irritating man she'd ever met, and she couldn't get him out of her mind. Would it be her fate to always be attracted to difficult man because of her past?

Before heading home, Ginny stopped in the teacher's lounge to retrieve the containers she'd brought with her lunch.

The minute she opened the door, Nancy Bennett, from the math department, called out, "Here comes the bride, ladies. Shall we all stand and bow?"

Leann Jennings, the Phys. Ed. Teacher, made the next comment. "I'll bow to any woman who can tame the chief, let alone the beast he calls Bear."

Ginny realized they were teasing and laughed. "Hey, Bear is a sweetheart, but I'm not sure if Brett is really so tamed yet."

"You don't want that man to be too tame, sweetie," Gloria Burnside, the history teacher said. "It takes half the fun out of it. The other half of the fun would be just seeing that man naked."

"This is really getting disgusting," Nancy added. "First you start out like teacher of the year. All the kids can talk about is how Ms. Silverfeather does this and what Ms. Silverfeather thinks about that. Then your husband gets on stage in front of the whole town and declares you the world's most perfect wife. The man is willing to even go hungry for you. I know all about men, honey, and that's a big concession."

Leann jumped in again. "I don't know who's more jealous, me or my husband, Glenn."

"There's only one way we'll be able to leach all your secrets out of you," Gloria said, "You'll have to come to the Women's Club meeting tomorrow night and let us stuff you with cookies and coffee until you beg for mercy and tell all."

Ginny suddenly stopped laughing. "Are you serious? You're really inviting me to the Women's Club meeting?" She knew what an honor this was in a small town like Three Trees. The Women's Club was almost a secret society.

"Well," Gloria answered, "actually we're much too jealous of you for that, but your mother-in-law requested you be allowed to attend. We'd look like total shits if we didn't agree. So, you get to supply the paper plates and cups. We don't trust you with baking yet."

"Yeah," Leann added, "when you become the perfect cook, we'll have to either run you out of town or kill you."

****

Ginny pulled into the drive at home and was surprised to see Brett's personal vehicle, an extended cab Dodge pickup, was sitting next to his county SUV. She hadn't seen him use it since she'd arrived. Several huge boxes were leaning against the barn by the garbage cans. Bear ran toward her from the back of the barn barking excitedly. When he stopped at her feet, she leaned down to scratch his scruff.

"Good news, Teddy Bear, I'm making new friends around here. Before you know it, we'll be throwing parties and backyard barbeques. Isn't it great?"

Bear barked in answer.

Inside the kitchen, Ginny found a sink full of dirty dishes. This wasn't like Brett at all. Had she entered into an alternate universe? Before she could finish the thought, she heard pounding from upstairs. Maybe he had finally decided to do something with the empty rooms up there. But why was he home so early?

When she reached the top step, Ginny found a huge pile of shopping bags from a department store. The closest store of that kind was in Valdosta. Had he been to work at all?

She peeked inside the room to the left, toward noises. Inside were two new desks, two new dressers, and a set of half constructed bunk beds. The mattresses were leaning against the wall and a new rug had been laid in the center of the floor.

Kyle Harvey grinned up at her from where he sat on the floor. "Welcome home, Mom!"

Cole Harvey poked his head out from behind the bed frame. "Did you bring me anything?"

Brett wiped the sweat off his forehead with his forearm. "Umm, Dove, we need to talk."

Chapter Fourteen

Brett walked out of his grandfather's hardware store at mid-morning to return to work. He'd wanted to tell the old man about the Harvey boys moving in to his house and maybe get a little advice on how to handle them. Poppy's only advice was to keep them busy as much as possible.

"Boys their age have a lot of energy to spend. Give them something constructive to spend it on, that they can take pride in," Poppy had told him.

Brett planned to bounce a few ideas off Ginny as to how they could do that. She was his partner in this venture, even if he had blindsided her with the job.

Ginny took the news like a champ. She didn't have all the reservations about the situation he'd started out with. As a matter of fact, she dug right in. She washed the few clothes they had and talked to them about making up the schoolwork they'd missed. She'd even given them each a haircut. She seemed as happy as a hen with new chicks. Making Ginny happy was one of his top priorities now.

It amazed Brett to see how four peoples' lives could change so drastically in just twenty-four hours. Yesterday morning the boys had been miserably anticipating a long stay in juvenile detention, but were grateful to have a regular meal. This morning, they'd left for school with full stomachs, new attitudes, and looking like members of the junior league. If their washing dishes last night hadn't surprised him enough, their making breakfast this morning had downright left him speechless. Who would have guessed they could cook?

Brett had seen both their parents sign them away to the state the day before, and both had made the same comment as they'd done it, "Good riddance to the useless brats." Neither had ever seen the value in their own offspring. It would be interesting to see what the boys would do with a little guidance and encouragement.

After the boys had gone to bed, Ginny had told Brett about her conversation in the teacher's lounge. She was so excited about being invited to the Women's Club meeting she'd literally bounced in her chair and made wild gestures with her hands as she spoke. She put him in mind of a little girl on Christmas morning. Her wide smile and the sparkle in her eyes had filled his heart, but at the same time it made his heart ache a little. Such a small sign of acceptance seemed like more than she'd ever expected.

Brett remembered the way the house sounded as he laid in his bed the night before. The boys' footsteps had padded across the floor in the room upstairs, the toilet had flushed, and someone had run water in the bathroom sink. Bear's tail thumped against the floor in the kitchen. Ginny hummed a soft tune as she rustled through her closet in the room next to his. These had been nice sounds to go to sleep by. These had been the sounds of a family settling in for the night. He'd slept like a baby knowing the family was together and safe.

"You look awfully happy for a man who's about to be unemployed, Silverfeather."

Brett looked up at the sound of Orville Dagget's voice. He was surprised to see Dagget wasn't alone. Actually he was more surprised to see the woman who held Dagget's arm. A woman he hadn't thought he'd ever see again.

Brett looked into Diana's overly made-up eyes,

and then scanned down to her too-low-cut blouse, her much too short skirt and her ultra high heeled boots. He had once thought of her as glamorous and exciting. Now he saw her as cheap and arrogant. How had he ever thought that this woman would make a good mother for his future children? He realized he wasn't mad at her for leaving him. It had actually been a blessing. He was mad at himself for being stupid enough to have ever fallen in with her.

They both smiled at him like two cats with a cornered mouse.

"Cat got your tongue, sugar?" Diana purred.

Brett hated being called sugar. "Sorry, I was just trying to remember...Oh yeah. How are you, Diana?"

Diana's smile faltered as her fingers dug into Dagget's arm.

Dagget came to her rescue by directing Brett's attention back to him. "Henrietta was speaking to Diana on the phone last week about how well the campaign is going. She decided to grace us with a visit. I was just taking her around to see her old friends and decided to stop in at the florist to order an arrangement for my mother's birthday."

Brett turned a smile toward Diana. "I didn't realize you were so close to the Daggets. What was it you used to call them?"

"Why don't you go on inside, Orville?" Diana said, before Brett could relay the list of childish nicknames she had given them. "I'd like a minute to catch up on old times with Brett."

Dagget looked back and forth between them with a suspicious scowl. Finally he shrugged and said, "All right Diana. I'll only be a minute."

She waited for Dagget to go inside and then turned to Brett with her smile back in place. "I hear you didn't waste any time replacing me, darling. How's married life treating you?"

Brett chuckled. "Did you honestly think you'd come back after a year and find me crying on a barstool over you, Diana? I moved on and I was lucky enough to find a woman who is truly irreplaceable. I've never been happier."

"I just can't imagine a man like you being happy with a little schoolteacher for very long. I even heard she's as white as the driven snow."

Brett smiled. "I had never imagined the surprises that can come in a little package. The fact that she's an educated, professional woman makes her more interesting to spend time with, when I'm not busy exploring those surprises. A man has to stop and rest every now and then you know. By the way, Diana, how's the modeling thing going? I haven't seen you on the front of any magazines yet."

"It's just a matter of time," Diana huffed. "I've been staying busy in New York. I just love New York."

"That's great," Brett said with forced sincerity. "I'm glad you're happy too. From the way our lives have taken opposite directions, it's a lucky thing we didn't try to stay together, isn't it? It would have been hell for both of us and I might have never found my Ginny. I can't imagine my life without her."

Diana's smile had become as tight and uncomfortable looking as a stretched out rubber band about to snap. "I promised Orville I'd help him pick out those flowers for his mother. I should get inside. Men are so inept at that sort of thing."

"You don't have to tell me about that. I never know what to get Ginny, but she always seems to be thrilled with anything I choose. Or maybe she just likes showing her appreciation so much that she doesn't care what I bring home. Either way, it's a winning situation for me." Brett enjoyed watching Diana squirm as he played the happy husband.

"How nice for you." Diana gave him a little wave

and disappeared inside the flower shop.

An uncomfortable thought occurred to Brett. Ginny was destined to find out Diana had returned to Three Trees for a visit. How would she feel about it? He shrugged the thought away. There wasn't any way to hold back the gossip, but at least Ginny wouldn't have any reason to cross paths with his former fiancée.

****

Ginny had had the best day she could remember at school, but something seemed to be off at the grocery store. As she walked down the aisles to gather the paper products she'd been asked to bring to the Women's Club meeting, people gave her strange looks. No one would look her directly in the eye, and they whispered as soon as they were behind her. She wished Julie was working so she could find out what was going on. Perhaps they were still talking about Brett's speech and the kiss he'd given her at the podium.

Whatever it was they were talking about, Ginny knew couldn't be too bad. She hadn't been arrested so far that week. She'd promised herself and Brett she'd stay out of trouble and become Three Trees' most upstanding citizen. How hard could it be?

Several women were gathered outside the First Baptist Church when Ginny parked her little blue bug in the parking lot. By the time she'd gathered her purse and grocery bags, they'd all gone inside. She checked her watch to make sure she hadn't arrived late and found she still had five minutes to spare. To her relief, another car pulled in to the lot. It was driven by Mia with Mrs. Silverfeather and Julie in tow.

Each of Brett's sisters greeted her with a warm hug before unloading plastic containers filled with fresh baked cupcakes.

The thought of the sugary treats made Ginny's

mouth water. She hadn't had any time for lunch because Cole and Kyle had wanted her to give them a quick rundown on the chapters they'd missed in their literature class. Of course they hadn't gone hungry. The boys had eaten while she talked and read passages to them. She had a feeling they were both making up for lost time with meals as well as classes. Afterward, their participation in the class discussion had made her proud. She felt she could really get used to this nurturing thing. Then a hideous thought crossed her mind. What if she had her own babies and then turned into her mother? Was it worth the risk?

"Dove," Mrs. Silverfeather greeted Ginny with a wide smile. "I want to introduce my new daughter to all my old friends. You've probably met everyone already, but I want to show off a little."

Ginny walked into the church with her mother-in-law's arm tucked into hers. Maybe, with this woman's influence, she could learn to be a good mother.

The large group of women seemed unusually quiet as they covered the buffet table with luscious looking desserts. Even Mrs. Silverfeather and her daughters looked around curiously. Finally the meeting was called to order by the tapping of a gavel.

Brett's sister, Mia, read the minutes from the last meeting when they had discussed a fund-raiser for new holiday decorations for the streets. They had decided to have a bake sale at the Heritage Day festival, which had gone well. The supplies would be purchased and turned over to the high school's electronics and woodworking department for construction.

Also, Mrs. Simmons had agreed to take pictures of the town to use in a calendar, which would be sold for a donation to the town library.

When asked if there was any new business to discuss, Mrs. Jenkins' hand popped up. "I propose we collect recipes for a cookbook to sell. We'll need money for new flowers along the curbs, come spring, and a hometown cookbook would make a nice holiday gift."

Everyone agreed the cookbook was a good idea. Ginny wanted to participate, but didn't have a clue what she could contribute. Mrs. Silverfeather whispered in her ear, "Brett makes the best venison and bean stew you've ever tasted. I'll bet he could be persuaded to share the recipe."

Ginny gave her mother-in-law's hand a slight squeeze to show her appreciation for the suggestion.

A moment later, a woman stood and waved to gain Mia's attention. Ginny had never seen her before. She seemed too flashy and pretentious to fit in among the others.

The woman cleared her throat. "I'd like to take the floor to discuss the woman's role in government elections, considering that voting day is fast approaching."

Several gazes discreetly swayed toward Ginny. She was confused until Mia spoke with an icy glare at the woman.

"We'll recognize Diana Rainflower as a guest speaker, since she's no longer a resident of Three Trees."

Ginny surveyed the woman's appearance more closely as she sauntered up to the front of the room. She was at least five-ten and thin, with long black hair teased to full volume. She wore theatrical makeup including false lashes and a white silk blouse filled with silicone. Her tiny leather skirt was a size too small and the above the knee pirate boots were tall enough to cause the wearer nosebleeds. This was the woman Brett had intended to marry. Diana was a far cry from the ordinary schoolteacher he'd gotten stuck with. Ginny wanted to hate her, but instead she felt plain, puny, and inadequate by comparison.

Diana let her gaze roam over her audience as she began, "As you know, women make up half of the voting population. The way we vote can make or break a candidate. While men often rely on heroics and grand gestures to form their decisions, we should use reason and logic. We should consider a candidate's loyalty, consistency, devotion, decisiveness, and decency." She gave Henrietta a warm smile. "Your candidate should have the ability to deliberate on an issue and decide what is best for his people, rather than acting on impulse. He should research every issue to decide the best course of action for all involved. He should also surround himself with the highest quality people, people who are above reproach."

She gave Ginny a scathing look. "Don't be blinded by charm and good looks, ladies. Too many of us make that mistake in our personal lives. Consider the candidate's *true* character when you go to the polls."

The audience applauded politely.

Ginny finally felt the hatred for Diana she'd expected at first sight. She wanted to punch her in the nose, but knew it would be the wrong thing for the town's most upstanding citizen to do.

Julie jumped to her feet. "I agree with most of what you say, Diana, but there are exceptions to some things.

"There are certain cases when we want a man who has proven he can be brave and capable of making snap decisions in times of crisis. I'd hate to think a person would have to deliberate very long or not trust his impulses when it came down to a life or death decision. I feel training and experience should also be considered.

"I know my candidate has the highest level of character and surrounds himself with high quality people, because his people are the people of Three Trees. You can't get any better than that."

The audience was still clapping loudly as Julie took her seat beside Ginny. Ginny hugged her tightly.

"You're my hero." Ginny whispered in Julie's ear.

"Thanks, but I think you already have one," Julie whispered back.

****

Ginny stood at the buffet table with the other Silverfeather women while her mother-in-law ladled fruit punch into cups for the women who didn't drink coffee.

"The Harvey boys are outside doing their homework at the picnic table," Marsha Silverfeather said. "I never thought I'd see the day. If you can turn those boys around, you're a better teacher than I ever dreamed."

"Let's see how it goes after the honeymoon period is over," Mia laughed.

"They agreed to fold up the chairs and help clean up after the meeting in exchange for a ride home," Ginny informed them. "From what I've been told, riding the bus is lame."

Mandy laughed. "It's lucky for them that you happen to work at their school."

"It's also lucky for them that Brett was in the courtroom yesterday and the two of you have such big hearts," Marsha added.

Ginny looked over the assortment of baked goods on the table. "I'm starving and this all looks so good. Do you suppose it would be all right if I sneak a couple things out for the boys? They never stop eating."

"Sure," Julie said, "just as long as you stay away

from Mrs. Simmons blueberry delights."

Ginny looked at the blueberry tarts covered in thick blue whipped cream. "They look decadent, what's wrong with them?"

"Well," Mia volunteered, "I don't know what she uses to make those things so blue, but they'll stain your teeth better than Rit. I had to use peroxide and baking soda for days to get it off after she pushed one on me last summer."

Ginny didn't know what Rit was, but it sounded serious. "I think I'm allergic to blueberries today." She chose two peanut butter cookies for herself and a chocolate cupcake for each of the boys. When she turned back toward Julie she saw that Diana appeared behind her sister-in-law.

"You may think you've won this round, Julie," Diana said in a smooth calm voice, "but don't underestimate my influence with the women in this town. I plan to stick around and watch Brett fall like a lead balloon."

Next, she turned to Ginny. "And if you're thinking of giving me any trouble, think long and hard, because I can make your life a living hell. You're only a novelty to Brett right now. Only a real woman will be able to keep him satisfied. You're just a cream puff."

"Back off, Diana," Marsha warned.

"Diana!" Mrs. Simmons scurried toward them. "It's so nice to see you again. You have to try one of my blueberry delights." She placed one on a plate and handed it to Diana. "Believe me honey, you won't soon forget them."

"Well, I'll be a monkey's uncle," Mrs. Silverfeather murmured as she watched them walk away. "She uses the damned tarts as weapons. Mia, what did you do to her last summer?"

"Oh, it looks delicious, thank you," Diana exclaimed. She gave the Silverfeather women a snarl over her shoulder and then took a big bite of blueberry delight.

****

Brett was pacing the front porch when Ginny and the boys got home. He sent Kyle and Cole to take care of the animals and asked Ginny to stay and talk with him for a moment. He looked apprehensive and sheepish as he leaned on the railing across from her rocking chair.

"I just got off the phone with my mother," he said. "It sounds like you had an interesting meeting."

"You must mean because your girlfriend was there," Ginny replied boldly.

"She's not my girlfriend. She's just…Diana."

"You were honestly going to marry her, Brett? What part of your body were you thinking with?"

"You have to remember, that all started five years ago. I had just gotten my sheriff's badge. I was feeling young, horny, and bulletproof. She stroked my ego."

"To say the least. Well, whatever she was, she seems pretty mad at you now, which also makes her mad at me…by association, I guess." Ginny paused to think about it. "Anyway, she called me a cream puff. I wanted to punch her right in the rhinoplasty."

"You noticed that too?" Brett chuckled.

"Yeah." Ginny gave a delicate snort. "I wonder if she bought the boobs at the same time. Do you get a discount for package deals?"

"I don't know, but she should have had a new personality implanted while she was at it."

As they laughed, Brett took Ginny's hand and pulled her out of her chair to stand between his knees. "I'm proud of you, Dove. Mom says you kept your cool and didn't return fire."

"It's Julie you should be proud of." Ginny played with the button on his shirt. "She stood up for you in front of all those women."

"I am proud of Julie, but she's only my sister." Brett pulled Ginny closer and nuzzled her neck. "I'd like to show you my pride in a more than brotherly way."

"I think your pride is growing." Ginny glancing down between them.

"Is this a private party?" Cole shouted as he and Kyle walked around the side of the house.

Brett's head fell down to shake in the way Ginny had come to recognize and love.

"We're the young, impressionable type you know," Kyle added. "If you're going to get busy, you should go in the bedroom or something."

"Get busy? Don't you two have homework to do?" Brett groused.

Cole grinned. "Nope, it's all done."

Kyle looked more thoughtful. "How come you each have a bedroom anyway? Don't married people usually sleep in the same bed?"

Ginny answered quickly. "Brett's shoulder isn't really healed yet."

"Besides that," Brett added, "it's none of your business."

Cole looked down and shuffled his feet. "Ya know, we're really sorry our pa shot you. We didn't mean for anybody to get hurt."

Brett stepped away from Ginny and put a hand on each boy's shoulder. "What happened wasn't your fault. You boys did the right thing that day. I hope you know that. Either one of you, or your parents, could have ended up in worse shape, if you hadn't called for help when you did. Don't be sorry for that. I know it took a lot of guts and I'm proud of you for doing it."

The boys looked at each other with a grin, silently celebrating the first time someone had shown pride in them. They started to go inside the

160

house, but then Kyle stopped and looked back. "You know, it's really been bugging me, Ms. Ginny. I could swear I've seen that lady at the meeting somewhere before. I just can't figure out where it was."

"There were a lot of women at the meeting, Kyle."

"I mean the one with the big hooters, tall boots and blue teeth." He walked into the house still looking bewildered.

Ginny pulled her shirt out and looked down inside it with a dejected expression. She was only a C cup.

"For what it's worth," Brett commented, "I think you're perfect just the way you are."

Ginny smiled. "Thanks, I needed that."

"Blue teeth?" Brett asked.

"I'll explain later."

Chapter Fifteen

It seemed to Ginny that Diana showed up everywhere she'd been during the next week. Diana was charming and attentive with the other citizens of Three Trees while she sneaked scathing glances Ginny's way.

One evening Ginny stopped at the grocery store with Cole and Kyle on her way home from work. The boys had huddled together to whisper as they stared at Diana in her outrageous outfit. Ginny could only imagine the comments they made to each other. After all, they were nearly grown males battling an overabundance of hormones. She worriedly wondered what she could say to warn them away from such heart crushing females. Maybe it was a subject better left for Brett to discuss with them. But then again, he'd once fallen under this exact woman's spell. Maybe it was just something a man had to learn, a coming of age, or rite of passage type thing.

The boys were doing extremely well in school and working hard to help out at home. When their shields of arrogance were down they revealed an amazing amount of maturity. Ginny supposed that had come from the hard life they led with their parents. Just running, laughing and acting like kids seemed to be new to them and she enjoyed watching them take pleasure in it.

On Friday afternoon, Ginny was glad to be coming to the end of her work week. Brett had planned to take time from the office to take the boys camping for the weekend. The outing was to be like an old-fashioned trail adventure. He'd arranged to bring two more horses from Poppy's place for the boys. They'd be cooking over an open fire and sleeping under the stars, only cowboys allowed...well, two cowboys and an Indian.

The last class had been dismissed and Ginny was just settling in to grade papers when the door of her mobile classroom was thrown open and Henrietta Dagget swept inside.

Henrietta was red in the face. Hanks of hair had come loose from her signature bun. She looked around the classroom like a bloodhound on a scent.

"Where are they?" Henrietta demanded, "Where are those loathsome, vile, cretins you've been harboring?"

****

Brett took a break from the last of his paperwork to refill his coffee cup in the bullpen. While there, looking out the large front window, a strange vehicle pulled up outside the door. It was an old station wagon spotted with rust and filled with worn boxes and overstuffed garbage bags.

The woman who emerged from the driver's seat was middle-aged, but haggard. Her hair was shoulder length and bleached to the point of looking like straw. The plaid shorts and pink tank top hung from nothing but skin and bones. Her white sneakers were dirty with holes worn in the toes. Her eyes were covered with large sunglasses even though the sky was overcast. Her thin, red painted lips drew down at the corners and held a lit cigarette. It appeared she had no teeth, real or otherwise.

She walked to the back of the vehicle where she unhooked and folded out a manual wheelchair that looked like it had seen better days. She rolled it to the passenger side to help a man into it.

The man was tall and looked as though he had once been athletic, maybe even a bodybuilder. His expression seemed to indicate irritation, resentment, and a long history of bad attitude. Although he was thin through his hips and legs now, the wheelchair had kept his tattooed arms and chest solid. Age and probably a lot of alcohol had added a flabby belly. He wore old jeans and a dirty undershirt. His brown hair was short and disheveled. He looked like he hadn't shaved in a few days.

The woman flicked her cigarette into the street, rolled the man inside, and walked straight up to Cora's desk.

"My name is Joyce Johnston and this here is my husband, Charlie Johnston. We heard that my daughter came down this way a few weeks back and we're looking for her." The woman looked around as though the environment made her nervous. "We figured this would be as good a place as any to start."

Brett's stomach did a jig while his heart leaped into double-time. "I'll handle this, Cora." He couldn't make himself touch these two people to offer a handshake, but he introduced himself and invited them into his office.

After shutting the door, the room filled with the odor of beer, cigarette smoke, and sweaty bodies. He opened the window and took a few deep breaths.

Brett struggled with the choice between avenging Ginny and keeping her and her secrets, safe. He had to admit there was really no choice. He'd have to play this with a detached cool manner. He sat behind his desk and looked at each of them, swallowing his anger.

"So, tell me how we can help you, Mr. and Mrs. Johnston."

"I went looking for my girl, Virginia," Joyce began, "and I was told by her neighbors up in Saginaw that she'd come down here. I want to find her."

Brett gripped his hands together on the top of his desk. "If she'd been living separately from you, Mrs. Johnston, I presume she's an adult. How long has it been since you've seen her?"

"Oh, we had a fallin' out years ago. Virginia is the promiscuous type, if you know what I mean. She was always flauntin' herself around my boyfriends, trying to steal 'em away from me. I finally had to turn her loose, but now I'm willin' to let bygones be bygones. Charlie here can tell you it's true. She tried seducin' him back when we was first livin' together. He was a strong handsome man back then, a tattoo artist by trade." Joyce lowered her voice. "That was back before his accident."

"That's enough, Joyce," Charlie butted in, "the man didn't ask for our life story." He turned to Brett with a sour look. "I guess it's been somewhere around ten years now. Why does it matter?"

Brett was still trying to swallow the ball of rage that had nearly choked him when Joyce said the word tattoo. He cleared his throat. "I'm just trying to get a sense of her age. How old is Virginia?"

The two looked at each other and then Joyce started counting her fingers. She had to start over twice.

"Well, I'm thirty-nine, so she must be around twenty-three."

Brett didn't know which was more disturbing; the fact that Ginny's own mother hadn't known her age, or that the old hag was only thirty-nine years old. It was appalling what drugs could do to a person. And thank heavens Ginny didn't resemble this woman in the least.

"So you haven't seen your daughter since she was thirteen? Why are you looking for her now? She's an adult and has a right to stay away, you know."

Joyce puffed up proudly. "We hear she went to

college and got a good job here. She's a teacher now. I hear teachers make pretty good money."

"I'm not sure if that answers my question. Let me repeat it." Brett took a deep breath. "Why are you looking for her?"

"Well," Joyce said with a sigh, "Charlie and me fell on hard times here lately. I know my little girl would want to put us up and help us out until we get back on our feet again."

Like hell, Brett thought. "I'll tell you what I can, Mr. and Mrs. Johnston." Brett didn't consider himself a good liar, but this time it was easy. "A young lady named Virginia came through town a few weeks ago. She was asking about a teaching job. While she was here she received an offer from a school out in New Mexico. Last I knew she was headed that way. I believe she said she was going to Albuquerque."

Brett walked them back to their car and watched as Charlie slid into the passenger seat. While Joyce reattached the wheelchair to the back, Charlie decided to be friendly with Brett. He was probably glad to have more distance between himself and the county jail.

"So, Sheriff, you on your way out to catch a bank robber or a killer or somethin'?"

"Nope." Brett smiled as he leaned close to the window. "I'm after a pedophile. You know what a pedophile is, don't you Charlie? It's a man who gets off on raping innocent little children." Brett paused, "Do you know anybody like that, Charlie?"

Charlie didn't say a word. An air of understanding passed between the two men.

In an even lower voice Brett asked, "Do you know what we do to pedophiles in my county, Charlie? We have a gator pit out behind the gas station. We figure they don't deserve the cost of a trial or a jail stay."

Brett straightened as Joyce walked up the other side of the car.

"Maybe we should find a place to stay the night and get a fresh start in the morning," she said.

"No!" Charlie yelled. He took a moment to lower his voice. "We still have enough daylight to make Alabama before we turn in."

Joyce cranked over the rumbling engine. "Well, I at least want to stop at the gas station and use the bathroom."

Charlie had begun to sweat. "You can hold it. Just drive."

As the car pulled away, Brett heard Joyce reply, "Easy for you to say, you've got a bag attached to your useless old pecker."

Finally, Brett could honestly smile. Some people did get what they deserved.

"Chief," Cora shouted from the door. "You have to get over to Clive Winters' office at the high school."

"Is Ginny all right?" Brett asked with instant concern.

"He says it's about those boys of yours."

My boys, Brett thought as a grin spread across his face again.

****

The school receptionist, Mrs. Parker, stood at the front counter outside Clive's door. She wrung her hands together and mumbled, "Oh lordy, lordy, it's bedlam, just pure bedlam. I don't know what we're going to do."

Brett didn't have a chance to ask what the problem was. He could hear Henrietta Dagget's voice screeching on the other side of the door. He just couldn't tell what she was saying.

When he opened the door he certainly heard Ginny's words loud and clear.

"You won't lay a finger on my boys without

167

getting past me first and I guarantee you, Henrietta, you'd rather take a razorblade bath than tangle with me."

This was a side of Ginny, Brett had never seen before, kind of scary, but he liked it. She stood with her face within inches of Henrietta's and she didn't appear to be backing up any time soon. He thought it was cute, the way her bottom lip stuck out when she scowled. Her little fists, all balled up, were about the size of plums, but he was betting she could put some power behind them when she was riled. And she was riled.

Brett circled her waist with one arm and pulled her off her feet to hold her against his side. "Slow down there, Tiger. I don't want to have to arrest you."

"You should arrest those repugnant juvenile delinquents right along with her." Henrietta pointed a pudgy finger to the corner where Cole and Kyle stood with wide eyes. "They're attempting to defame a sweet, innocent young woman."

"Mrs. Dagget," Clive cut in, "you've exceeded your boundaries. Go to your office and let me handle this." Next he turned to the boys. "You two can catch the bus home and stay there for the next week. You're suspended...again."

"I swear, Mr. Winters, we didn't doctor that picture," Kyle said.

"You can look it up yourself on bedroombeauties.com," Cole added, "we found it months ago...by accident."

Henrietta harrumphed loudly.

"I said go, Mrs. Dagget!" Clive shouted.

Brett watched her close her office door before he let the boys leave and then he sat Ginny in a chair. "What's going on here, Clive? Why are my boys being suspended?"

"Distribution of inappropriate materials," Clive

answered as he held up a full color, nearly pornographic picture.

It was a web site page that had been printed on plain paper from a computer. Probably his own home computer, Brett thought.

In the picture, Diana stood in a seductive pose wearing a large feathered headdress and a barely-there buckskin bikini top and g-string. The bold letters across the top read, Indian Princess, Diana Dancing-Tongue, does it all. Along the side was a video menu listing every type sex act known to man...or woman. The web address Cole had mentioned was clearly printed along the bottom.

"Do you think the boys found a way to fabricate that picture?" Ginny asked.

"No," Clive answered. "I remember when Diana got that little scar on her shoulder."

Brett cleared his throat. "The rose tattoo on her, umm, derriere is also authentic. What's even worse," he pointed to a place in the background, "her mother wove that blanket for the fair a few years ago. It won a blue ribbon."

"Nice blanket," Clive quipped. "Now it's being appreciated inside every boy's locker in this school."

"Since you have so many copies, I'll just keep this one." Brett folded the paper and placed it in his shirt pocket.

"Hey!" Ginny objected.

Brett looked at her seriously. "I'll have to turn this in to the Council of Elders. Our lawyers will have to look into shutting this down. This is not the way we expect our people to represent us."

Clive nodded. "It'll be hardest on her parents. They were both born and raised here. Now they'll want to move away."

Brett shook his lowered head. "I'll talk to the boys about the backlash this is going to cause."

"Now hold up, Brett," Clive interrupted. "They

shouldn't have been on that web site and they damn sure shouldn't have passed these pictures to school. That's what you need to talk to them about. But they're not at fault for the content. Diana owns that, all by herself.

****

Ginny had glanced into her rearview mirror a hundred times on her ride home. Brett's huge SUV stayed right on her tail the whole way. Under his sunglasses and hat was a very grim expression.

She wondered how Brett would handle the boys' discipline. Men that shouted, pushed, or hit tended to make her nervous. She'd been on the receiving end too many times. Her mother had always been too zoned out to notice, let alone care. This time, however, these were her boys, and she did care. She'd realized in Clive's office that she felt a tremendous sense of protectiveness for Kyle and Cole.

Taking on Henrietta Dagget was one thing; bucking Brett's authority would be another.

She and Brett stepped out of their vehicles at the same time. As Brett walked toward her, Ginny thought again about what a big man he was. Her mother had always preferred big men. "They'll keep you safe," Joyce had said. Ginny hadn't found that to be true.

"Do you have your feathers back in order, Mother Hen?" he asked.

"Wh-what do you mean?"

"Dove." Brett put his arm around her shoulders. "I was impressed by the way you stood up for the boys, but you really have to keep control of that temper."

Just then Poppy's truck and horse trailer rattled into the drive. He'd come to deliver the two horses for the camping trip, but it appeared he had picked up an extra. He drove slowly, holding Havoc's reins through the window. Bear was running up from behind, barking excitedly.

"It looks like someone tried to steal your mount, Little Chief. I guess they didn't know what a cantankerous cuss he can be."

Havoc stood calmly and allowed Brett to look him over even though he had recently worked up a sweaty lather. He was well and fully saddled with a plastic grocery bag tied around his saddle horn.

Poppy unloaded the first of his two pintos. He handed Ginny the lead rope as he walked back up the ramp for the second. "I guess we'd better see if Cinnamon is in her stall."

"Not likely," Brett replied as he looked inside the plastic bag. "Our horse thieves were also making off with peanut butter sandwiches and a box of Pop-tarts."

"Do you think it was Kyle and Cole?" Ginny asked.

Brett nodded. "They probably thought they'd be in for the brand of punishment their daddy would've doled out. I imagine they've felt the business end of his belt a few times. The problem we have now is that Havoc is known to throw strange riders. One of the boys may be hurt."

"Oh, good lord," Ginny gasped, "how are we going to find them?"

"Easy." Brett swung into Havoc's saddle. He leaned down toward his dog and commanded, "Go back, Bear."

Poppy leaped onto the bare back of the second Pinto and raced after the retreating dog. He cried out three ear piercing whoops as his hair flew like silver wings behind him.

The call Brett sent out as he followed was more like the caw of a hawk, but just as loud and sharp.

****

Brett found the boys slowly walking back up the

Sandra Dailey

trail they'd taken south, leading Cin between them. Kyle was covered in red dust and looked mad enough to eat nails.

"That dang fool horse of yours went crazy and threw me," he shouted.

"That's what happens when you take a man's horse without asking," Brett shouted back. "Nobody rides Havoc but me. That's a rule."

"Back in the old days, horse thieves were hung." Poppy dismounted and pointed to a fallen tree at the side of the trail. "Sit down over there and I'll have a look at you."

"Are you like a medicine man, Poppy?" Cole asked.

"Yep..." Poppy ran his hands over Kyle's head and neck and gently turned his head in every direction.

"Are you gonna dance around a fire, shakin' a rattle, and chantin' weird noises?" Kyle asked suspiciously.

"Maybe," Poppy answered as he looked into each of Kyle's eyes and directed them with his finger.

After every muscle was tested and bone was felt, it was determined Kyle had bumped his head and had the wind knocked out of him...period.

"Well, at least it won't keep you from seating a horse this weekend," Brett commented.

"You mean we still get to go campin'?" both boys asked in unison.

"Oh yeah," Brett answered. "We'll go camping all right. You two are in for two days of hard labor while listening to every word I have to say."

****

The boys were sound asleep upstairs and Bear had found a cool place on the kitchen floor to lie down.

Brett's shower turned off. Ginny looked out at the full moon through his bedroom window. She

172

tried reining in her nerves but her mind kept wandering. Would he be mad she'd invaded his private sanctum? Would he laugh and think her ridiculous? Would he look at her with pity or distaste and try finding a nice way to let her down easy?

The water stopped in the bathroom sink. She pulled the silky robe tighter around herself. Would she have time to get out of the room without his knowing she'd ever been there? Did she really want to?

The bathroom door opened, spilling bright light into the room around Brett's large dark silhouette. As he slowly approached, his naked body was touched by the soft blue glow from the window. Magnificent was the only word that came to Ginny's mind. The man exuded strength and power with every movement. Every part of his body was a work of art. Every piece, collected in perfect proportion to create a masterpiece.

In spite of all the phrases she'd rehearsed, Ginny was speechless.

Brett took the towel from around his neck and fastened it around his waist to cover himself. "Is everything all right, Ginny?" he asked softly.

"Yes...yes, everything is fine. I just wanted to say...thank you."

"Are you talking about the boys today?" He stepped even closer. "You know they aren't exactly off the hook."

"No, I know, but I'm not talking about the boys. I'm talking about Sunday afternoon...at the lake. You made me feel so...wonderful." Ginny let her robe slide to the floor.

Brett looked down at her green lace bra and thong panties. They were the exact color of her eyes. He ran one finger under the thin strap on her shoulder. "Ah baby, please don't tell me this is about gratitude."

"No," she said as she ran her hands over the hard plains of his chest. "This is about want. I want you, Brett."

Brett shook his head. His eyes squeezed shut and his teeth clenched. "I made a promise to you Dove."

In one swift tug Brett's towel was in Ginny's hand. "Your honor is safe with me, Chief. I'm not going to do anything to you that you haven't done to me."

Chapter Sixteen

Brett opened his left eye to look at the clock. It was 2:03 a.m. He felt limp and cozy. Ginny's steady breathing was like a lullaby. Nothing could pull him away from her...except the call of nature. Dammit.

After taking care of urgent business, Brett returned to the side of the bed. He looked down at her, sleeping like a contented baby. Her soft pouty lips brought back erotic memories from only hours before. The scraps of green lace she still wore teased his imagination. Every inch of his body wanted to reach out and touch hers. But it wouldn't be fair. She'd stayed in his bed because she trusted him, and a big part of trust was keeping promises.

Brett sat in a chair by the window. He couldn't take his eyes off her. He smiled ruefully. He'd thought he was such a tough guy. Then a little blonde from Saginaw came along and showed him what tough really was. He'd given himself a yearlong pity party just because he'd gotten dumped, when it was probably the best thing that could have happened to him.

His mood sobered when he thought about what she'd been through to make her so tough.

Had he ever shown his mother or Poppy the appreciation they deserved for raising him in a safe, secure, loving family. He knew he'd never put it into words. Maybe it was about time he did.

He'd never had to struggle for food, shelter, or personal safety. It made his heart ache to remember that Ginny hadn't had the same advantages.

The image of her bright, warm smile filled his

mind. He shook his head. How had she survived and turned out to be so amazing? She'd put herself through school and become the best damned teacher Three Trees ever had. Someday she'd be a terrific wife and mother. But, would she be his wife, for real? Would she be the mother of his children? Brett wanted that, more than anything else in the world.

At that moment his cell phone rang.

"Chief, you need to get over to the County Line Motor Lodge, ASAP," Pamela Armstrong, the night dispatcher, barked. "Carl and Larry should be getting there right about now and Lisa and Beau are right behind them."

Brett ran to the closet and grabbed his clothes as he spoke. "The motor lodge is out of our jurisdiction. What's going on?"

"The GHP are taking down a huge prostitution bust right now," Pamela informed him. "But most of them have been called away to a pileup out on the interstate. Their timing got screwed up by a jackknifed tractor-trailer. They need backup and extra cars.

"You'll be lucky to beat the media. They'll be more interested in the hookers then those poor people in the crash," she added.

"As long as it's turning into a circus, you may as well call my brother Jake and give him a heads-up, but don't tell him it came from me."

When Brett folded his phone closed, a sleep tousled Ginny was looking back at him. More than anything, he wished he could crawl back into the bed.

"What's going on?" she asked.

"The GHP just needs a little help with transport, nothing to worry about. I should be back in a couple of hours."

Ginny got up quickly and threw on her robe. "I'll heat some coffee while you get dressed."

****

Five minutes later Ginny met Brett at the foot of the stairs with a ham sandwich and a travel mug of warmed coffee left over from dinner. Seeing him in his uniform still caused her breath to catch.

"Drive carefully and come home safe," she said.

"I'll be home soon, Dove, and when I do we need to talk. I've been thinking a lot about our relationship."

Had he actually said the word, relationship? Ginny hadn't expected to ever hear that. Not after what he'd been through with Diana. Maybe it was time to talk, she thought. Her feelings for Brett were growing and it wasn't fair to keep him in the dark about her past.

"Brett, there's a lot of things about me you don't know."

He looked her in the eye when he shook his head. "No Ginny, I know just about everything. I got your records from Michigan, the police, the hospital. All I can say right now is...I'm sorry."

Before he could finish, two heads popped over the railing above them.

"What's going on?" Cole asked. "Why are you dressed for work?"

"What about our campin' trip?" Kyle followed.

"Everything's already packed. I'll be home in time to go. Get some more sleep." He looked back down at Ginny. "You too. We'll talk later."

The last words Ginny could remember hearing before the front door closed were I'm sorry. He was sorry. He had found out about her parents, the men, the pregnancy and he was sorry. She couldn't blame him. He'd led a clean life. He was the town sheriff. Why would he want to become involved with a person like her? They'd gotten too close...and he was sorry.

She should have known he'd run a background

check on her. Still, it seemed so invasive. She knew he had trust issues, but why hadn't he checked her out before he'd sent for her? Why hadn't he done it before they'd gotten married...before she'd made a fool of herself in his bed?

Ginny walk into the guestroom and began to pack. She figured Brett would get through the election. No one would blame him for separating from her when they found out what she was. He'd probably even get sympathy votes. She'd find a place to stay where she could still fulfill her obligation to the school, if they'd still have her. After that, she just didn't know.

She'd wait to leave until Brett and the boys had gone camping. She couldn't stand the thought of saying good-bye. Brett could explain, however he chose. It was the coward's way out, but worse things had been said about her.

At 5:15 a.m., Brett bounced up the porch steps looking wide awake. She felt like a wrung out mop.

The boys had all four horses tied to the porch railing and were ready for their trip to the woods. They were each riding one of the pintos, while Brett rode Havoc and Cin carried their gear.

She'd had reservations about the boys taking their twenty-two rifles, but they explained they'd had the rifles since they'd been twelve-years-old. The woods could be dangerous with snakes and wild animals. They also admitted they were hoping Brett would give them target practice with his expert instruction.

Kyle told her he'd been thinking about a career in law enforcement and Cole was considering the military. Sometimes, she forgot how close they were to becoming adults. She had just gotten them and they were already preparing to leave. Tears stung her eyes. It was just as well, under the circumstances. The court had turned the boys over to

Brett and the three of them would do just fine without her.

It only took Brett five minutes to be changed into jeans, a T-shirt, and old boots. His straw cowboy hat was in his hands when he approached her. "Are you sure you'll be all right here alone until tomorrow night?"

"I've lived alone for a long time," she said sadly.

Ginny could tell by the look on his face Brett didn't want to leave. She couldn't imagine why. Maybe he was ready to have it out with her. She doubted he'd say anything in front of the boys and they were staying close to his heels. They were anxious to go.

"Did you put all the bad guys in jail, Chief?" Cole asked.

"Yeah," Brett said, reluctantly turning away from Ginny, "but you know how it is. They were probably out before I could get home."

"What all happened?" Kyle asked.

"I can't discuss an open case, especially when the case belongs to someone else. I imagine it'll be all over the news by the time we get back. For now, I just want a nice, quiet, work free weekend."

"Yeah," Cole said as he mounted his horse and took Cin's reins, "we'll be doin' all the work this weekend."

Kyle mounted his horse as well. "Did you have to remind him?"

"I guess you'd better get going," Ginny said.

"Do you remember what I said this morning?" Brett asked.

"Yes, I remember."

When she didn't say more, an odd expression crossed his face. She supposed it was a look of regret or apology.

"Listen, I'm going to let Bear run with us as far as the campsite, and then I'll send him back to you. I don't like leaving you by yourself."

Ginny wanted to tell him not to bother, but she couldn't. "Okay."

This time she didn't wait to see them off. She walked into the house and closed the door without another word.

It only took Ginny an hour and a half to thoroughly clean the house and do all the laundry. She sat at the kitchen table and stared at a blank piece of paper. It only seemed right to leave a note so Brett wouldn't think she'd just gone into town. It was best he know right away that he didn't have to wait for her. He'd probably be relieved not to have to end things between them himself.

The phone rang. It wasn't her phone anymore and Ginny was reluctant to answer, but then she saw the caller ID. It was Gloria Burnside, the school history teacher.

"Have you seen the news? Turn on Channel 12. This is the juiciest news we've had in town since...well, that picture of Diana Rainflower was pretty juicy, but this is even better. That husband of yours looks just as good on TV as he does in real life. Do you think the camera really does add ten pounds?"

By the time Ginny got to the living room and punched the remote for the TV the story was almost over. A freeze-framed picture in the background showed Brett, backlit by red and blue lights. He was sporting a severe scowl as he was handcuffing a skinny old man wearing only a bed sheet. Then she looked closer and couldn't believe her eyes. She listened to the end of the story.

"In total there were nineteen arrests, ten women for prostitution, and the nine men who had hired them. Among the men was defense attorney, Orville Dagget, who is currently running for sheriff in the town of Three Trees. Mister Dagget is also charged with trying to bribe a law enforcement officer. Ironically, it was the current sheriff of Three Trees who had the honor of placing Mister Dagget under arrest. It appears Sheriff Silverfeather may run unopposed in this year's election."

Gloria giggled on the other end of the line. "Do you suppose it was good old Orville who paid for a double? What will Henrietta say?"

The two women joked about the arrest for a few more minutes before they hung up. Ginny felt relieved she wouldn't have to worry about the impact that their break up would have on Brett's chances for re-election.

She looked at the suitcases she'd left by the door and decided to load them into her car before she went back to write the note.

Outside, Bear was lying under the edge of the porch in the shade. Brett had sent him back to her as promised. If there was one thing she could say about Brett, he always kept his promises. Obviously, she couldn't say the same about herself.

She wondered if Brett would take her betrayal as badly as he took Diana's. No, he'd only known her for a few weeks. She hadn't meant as much to him as Diana had. Despite what he'd said, he had asked Diana to marry him. He'd intended them to be lifelong partners.

After the revelation of Diana's chosen profession, she wouldn't be making a repeat performance in his life. She'd probably never have the nerve to step foot in Three Trees again. But some extremely lucky woman would come along one day. It was just as well Ginny got out of the way. She wanted to put miles between herself and Three Trees before Brett fell in love. That was one thing she knew would destroy her.

All Ginny's worldly belongings fit neatly into the back seat of her little blue VW bug. What did that say about her life? She'd never really thought of herself as the type to settle down until she met Brett. But, here she was on the road again...alone. Maybe that's just the way it was meant to be. After the way she'd grown up she shouldn't have allowed herself to hope for more.

Suddenly Bear started barking.

She brought her head up and turned at the sound of a car slowly approaching the house. It was a brown, late model Olds Cutlass. She couldn't recall ever seeing it before, but many people in town chose to walk from place to place. It was probably another person who wanted to talk about the big sting out at the motor lodge.

As the car got closer, Bear's growls and barks grew more vicious. He came over to stand with his rump against her legs. Every hair down his back stood on end and his ears flattened against his head. The chill that ran up Ginny's spine kept her from trying to calm the dog. Instead she wrapped both hands around his thick leather collar to keep him near her.

Ginny was shocked and frightened to see Orville Dagget step from the car. Shocked because she hadn't believed he would be released from jail so quickly and frightened because of the wild look in his blood-shot eyes. He stood silently staring at her. The car door stood open as a barrier between them.

"If you're looking for Brett, he's not here," Ginny said as she struggled to control Bear.

"I'll wait," Dagget growled.

"That's not a good idea, Mr. Dagget. I was just getting ready to leave and Bear doesn't seem to want your company."

Dagget was breathing hard and sweating. "You're not going anywhere, and neither am I. Not until I'm finished with Silverfeather. As for the dog, you must have a way to chain him up or something.

I would advise you to do it immediately."

Ginny's heart pounded painfully, but she refused to show fear. "Mr. Dagget, you cannot come onto my property and order me around. If you don't leave immediately I'll call the police."

Dagget laughed. Ginny couldn't believe he actually laughed. "Do you think it matters anymore? If you can't do something about that dog, I can."

Dagget's arms came up to rest on the top of his car door with both hands folded around the handle of a gun. Ginny didn't know much about guns, but she could see this one was different from Brett's. It was longer and thinner with a revolving bullet chamber. It wouldn't hold as many bullets as Brett's, but did it really matter? It would only take one to kill Bear or anyone else he decided to turn it on.

"No...don't please, don't." Ginny wanted to cry. Memories flowed through her mind of times when she felt helpless, times when she was forced to do things she didn't want to do. Even in those times, she'd never been threatened with a gun. She wasn't sure if she'd survive this time.

Bear's barking stopped. He lowered himself into position to lunge. His had became a low steady rumble. He was her only protection, but she couldn't stand the thought of him being hurt or killed for her. She wished Brett had never sent him.

"Bear!" she shouted.

The dog snapped his eyes toward her and then back to Dagget.

Ginny pulled his collar as hard as she could. "Go back, Bear, go back!"

When Ginny released his collar, Bear raced past the barn and across the field. Ginny watched his rapid escape. A shot rang out, but the dog didn't slow down. Dagget had missed him. She was flooded with a sense of relief until she saw that the gun was now trained on her.

Chapter Seventeen

Brett relaxed under a wide oak tree while the boys settled the horses, set up camp, collected wood, and started a small fire. He'd intended to use this time to torture Cole and Kyle with a daylong lecture, but he just couldn't seem to work up the energy. He'd stayed awake late the night before, with Ginny's help. Then he'd been called out in the wee hours to work.

He didn't regret the loss of sleep. Ginny had treated him to all kinds of surprises. Cuffing and shoving Dagget into the back of his car was the icing on the cake. But now, turning off his mind for a nap was impossible.

The peculiar way Ginny responded to him this morning wouldn't leave him alone. She'd been extremely open the night before, but in the light of day, she'd been as closed off as a brick barn with no doors. Maybe she'd just been reciprocating his attentions and wasn't really that into him.

He shook his head. He was starting to sound like a schoolgirl, suffering her first crush.

Brett noticed when Cole stopped dead in his tracks and looked all around the area.

"Does anyone else hear that?" Cole asked as he slowly reached for the rifle he'd leaned against a tree trunk.

They all fell silent for a moment before Brett answered. "I'm not sure, but I think that sounds like Bear."

"A bear?" Kyle asked with alarm.

"No, I mean my dog, Bear."

A moment later Bear broke through the stand of trees sheltering the camp from the direction of the house several miles away. His coat was slick with perspiration; ropes of drool flew around his face as he barked hysterically. He had been running and barking for so long his voice had almost been reduced to a sharp whistle. They all watched in stunned silence as the dog ran in circles around the camp.

Finally Brett called, "Slowdown boy! Come here."

"That dog's gone mad!" Cole shouted, still holding his rifle at the ready.

"Do you think he got poisoned or bit?" Kyle asked.

"I don't know." Brett grabbed the dog by his massive head. "He's bleeding."

Brett separated the hair on Bears right shoulder and found a deep groove cut out of his hide.

The boys inched closer for a look. "What'd he get into?" one of them asked.

"Somebody took a shot at him." Brett stood to slide his personal handgun from the holster on his belt. He checked the clip, chambered a round and returned it to his holster.

"Maybe he spooked a hunter," Kyle suggested.

Brett released Havoc from the cross rope he'd been tied to and leaped onto his bare back. "He still would have headed to the house. I told him to go home.

You boys stay here until I get back. Don't move from this spot. Bear, you stay too!" As Brett spurred Havoc toward home he sounded his three sharp hawk calls.

"The chief's on the warpath," Cole stated in awe.

"I sure wouldn't want to be that hunter." Kyle added.

****

Dagget held the gun to Ginny's head as she pulled the wooden side chair to the center of the living room floor. After she sat, he yanked the cords from the curtain rods and forced her to tie her own ankles to the chair legs and her left wrist to the arm. When she made a knot too loose or slowed the process, he hit her across the face with the back of his closed fist. Because of her shaking hands, she took several blows.

The monster from Ginny's past was back. Her old defense kicked in automatically. The little girl inside her brain hid in a dark corner. Years ago she'd thought death might be preferable, but now she wanted to live. Brett had helped her realize her dreams. He'd shown her that the world could be a wonderful place.

A bruise on her cheekbone swelled and blood trickled from her split bottom lip, but she didn't make a sound.

Dagget only put the gun down in order to tie her other wrist. As soon as he knew she was securely bound, the gun was again in his hand and pointed at her.

Looking down the barrel of the gun, Ginny knew she had to try to save herself. "I don't understand why you're doing this. You haven't done anything bad enough to go to prison, until now. If you just untie me and leave, no one will ever know you were here. I won't tell anyone. I'll just tell Brett I fell down the stairs. He knows I'm clumsy. He'll believe me. There's no sense in ruining your entire life over one lapse of judgment."

"Do you honestly think that's all this is about?" Dagget sneered. "My life was ruined as soon as I moved to this lousy town. It was always Silverfeather's fault. He's humiliated me for the last time."

"Brett hasn't done anything he wasn't required

to do," Ginny argued.

"You don't know anything," Dagget yelled. "He's embarrassed me every time we've been in a courtroom together. My success rate has dropped to less than fifty percent. He's always collecting all these witnesses and physical evidence for the prosecution. Nobody can be that good. I know he must fabricate most of the stuff he finds, but I can't prove it."

"Maybe he's just good at his job," Ginny said.

"Why? Because he's young and handsome? The stupid hicks in this town follow him as if he was the new Messiah. They all talk about how smart and good-looking he is. I hear it all the time. Even my own wife stares at him when she thinks I'm not looking. Now I'm losing her too, because of him. He could have covered for me this morning. He's covered for you plenty of times. Instead he had to take me out of that motel, nearly naked, in front of the whole world. Can you imagine how my wife is reacting to all this? She's leaving me." Dagget punched his own thin chest. "I've put up with that prissy old cow for twenty-five miserable years. And now, when I need her, she's leaving me."

Ginny couldn't hold back her next comment. "Perhaps the prostitutes had something to do with that."

Dagget hit Ginny hard on her head with the butt of his gun and she nearly blacked out. The pain was like an explosion that wouldn't recede. Colored pinpoints of light sparkled in her vision.

"Shut up, just shut up. You're no better than he is. You're just an extension of him. Henrietta has told me all about how the students and even other teachers follow you, as if you were the Pied Piper."

Dagget began pacing in front of her. His look of loathing had morphed into an expression of insane hatred. "It was bad before, but much worse now. It's like a form of mind control, probably to do with all that Indian mumbo jumbo. I'd bet every Silverfeather in town is in on it. They're everywhere, you know, all over town."

Ginny began wondering if he was still speaking to her. He acted as though he'd forgotten she was there.

But he hadn't. He swung back to look at her. "This was supposed to be my town. I've worked hard for it, and I deserve it. Now he's ruined everything. I'll get him back though. First, I'll kill you, just a little at a time, slowly. He'll know I made you suffer. He's a supercop. He'll be able to tell. After I'm finished, I'll burn this fancy house to the ground." Dagget looked around with excitement. "Built by his own two hands and destroyed by mine. I want him to see that, before I kill him. But first, you."

Dagget raised his gun and fired.

****

At the sound of a shot; Brett threw himself against his large bedroom window and landed in the shattered glass.

By the time he reached the other end of the hallway, Dagget was behind Ginny's limp body, facing him. His knobby fist held her head up by her hair. An old rusty revolver in his other hand was pressed against her temple. The cuts and bruises on her face and the bullet hole seeping blood on her shoulder caused pure hot rage to surge through Brett.

"You came to the party earlier than expected, but that's all right. It'll be more fun having you here." Dagget smiled triumphantly.

"Don't look so worried. She only fainted. I'll wait for her to come to before I put the next bullet in her. Where should it go?" Dagget lowered the barrel of the gun to Ginny's thigh. "How about right here?"

Brett raised both of his hands with his own gun

pointed toward the ceiling. "This is between me and you, Dagget. Let Ginny go. She hasn't done anything to hurt you."

"She makes you happy, and that's enough to make me hate her. Besides, I want you to see what I do to her, before I kill you, Silverfeather." Ginny moaned and Dagget pulled her hair hard. "I'm not letting either of you go."

"Think about it Dagget, you're using a small caliber gun with old ammunition. I can tell, because the bullet didn't have the power to go all the way through. That gun only holds six. You've used at least two. It's my guess you haven't cleaned it in a long time. It could jam up and blow your hand off the next time you pull the trigger." Brett was bluffing. He didn't know how old the bullets were or when the gun had last been cleaned. He certainly couldn't predict if it would jam, but he was encouraged by the confused look on Dagget's face.

"Let Ginny start walking toward town. This will all be over by the time she reaches help. You could be miles away by then."

Dagget's eyes darted from side to side as he thought. "Okay, Silverfeather, I'll make you a deal. I'll let her go if you hand over your gun and stay behind."

"Don't do it Brett," Ginny groaned. "Just shoot him. He's crazy."

Dagget jerked on Ginny's hair again. "He won't do that. He knows I'll kill you before I go down."

The gun barrel dug into Ginny's temple. Anger rushed through Brett's veins. On their wedding night he'd told her she'd always be safe with him. Dagget would pay for this.

"It doesn't matter," Ginny said. "I don't mean anything to him."

"You're wrong, Ginny," Brett said, as he slowly inched toward the fireplace, put his gun on the mantel, and placed his hands behind his head. "You're my Dove. You mean everything to me. Even Dagget knows that. Get out of the house and trust me to follow you." To Dagget he said, "Untie her and let her get through the door, then I'll step away."

"You've still got an advantage," Dagget said. "Get on your knees."

After Brett lowered himself to his knees, Dagget released Ginny's hand that he had tied and told her to untie the rest. He kept his gun aimed at Brett as she quickly fumbled with the knots.

She looked imploringly at Brett when she was finished, but he only gave her a slight nod. Not knowing what else to do, Ginny walked to the door and opened it. A deep voice spoke from the hallway. "Put the gun down or die, Dagget."

When Dagget swung around to face Beau Stevens, Brett let the bone handle of his war knife drop from his sleeve and into his hand. He waited for Dagget's gun hand to rise. In the next second the knife flew from his fingertips. The horrified look on Dagget's face proved that he knew he'd lost the battle. The blade was long enough to reach his heart.

****

Brett called Beau over to the ambulance when he saw him heading toward his car.

"Listen, Beau, I appreciate the way you handled things in there. You held back until Ginny was out of harm's way. That was good police work."

Beau turned a little red. "Heck Chief, I knew that if Miss Ginny got hurt because of me, you'd have my hide hung on your office wall. But thanks for calling me to back you up. It feels good to know that you trust me after the last time."

Brett gave him a slap on the shoulder. "If I didn't trust you, Beau, I would have taken your badge when you offered it to me."

He turned back to the back doors of the

ambulance, where the boys were hovering. "I thought I told you guys to stay at the camp until I got back."

Cole looked contrite. "Once Bear rested up a while he started actin' a little crazy again."

Kyle stepped in. "We decided to follow him and find out what was goin' on."

"Well, now you can follow him right out to the barn and get the chores done while I'm at the hospital with Ginny. You still owe me some hard labor."

"I guess we're still in trouble then," Cole said. "I was hopin' you'd forget about that."

"For now, I'll just leave you with two words— parental controls. You'll know what they mean soon enough."

Then, he remembered something he'd seen earlier. "Before you do the chores, though, you can take the bags out of Ginny's car. Take them to my room and I'll unpack them when I get home."

"We gotta roll, Chief," Tommy Lane called from the driver's seat.

Ginny looked stunned when he joined her inside the ambulance. "Are you really going to move me into your room?"

"Of course I am," Brett answered. "You're my wife. I figure you'll be healed up right about the time my thirty days are over."

"But I thought you were sorry about all this. You said you were this morning."

Brett looked confused, and then it hit him. "I didn't mean I was sorry about us. I meant I was sorry for what you'd been through. And I wanted to tell you that none of it matters to me because I love you."

"You do? You think this could actually work between us?"

"It has to." Brett kissed the corner of her swollen

mouth. "We already have matching bullet wounds. "While yours is healing up, we'll have plenty of time for the talk I mentioned. I want to get to know you, Mrs. Silverfeather."

Epilogue

One year later

Ginny watched the orange sparks from the campfire float into the sky and turn black on the soft breeze. She and Brett had been back to this spot several times since their wedding night, but tonight was more special than the first.

Today marked their first wedding anniversary. Neither of them had ever entertained the thought of ending their arrangement. Not since the day Orville Dagget shot her. Not since the first time Brett told her that he loved her. She hadn't believed at the time that any emotion could be as overpowering as the love she felt for him then, but this day had proven her wrong.

Standing in a circle of his people, Brett promised to be her partner, friend, and lover. He promised to always be patient and gentle with her and put their family above all else. If there was one thing in the world Ginny believed, it was that Brett took his words seriously and never broke his promises...not even when she begged him to.

Lying next to her, Brett interrupted her thoughts. "You're awfully quiet. Are you rethinking your lesson plan before school has even started?"

"No," Ginny replied, "but I am wondering how difficult it's going to be, getting through it all."

Brett turned onto his side to face her. "I thought everything went well last year, after Henrietta Dagget moved back to Ohio, at least. Every teenager in town is excited about the drama club you're putting together. And, the boys are looking forward to starting their junior year, especially now that they have the old car fixed up. It kept them busy all summer."

Ginny nodded, but kept a worried expression. "Cole and Kyle have come a long way since we took legal guardianship of them. They're truly part of our family now. How do you think they'll feel if we have a son of our own? Won't our baby inherit the next place in line as the band's chief?"

Brett gave her an assuring smile. "Poppy says the boys are doing well in their customs and traditions lessons. They already know the order of things. They'll hold an important place in the band, as their brother's advisors. They'll help him learn to track, hunt, ride and all that, as well."

"What if we have a daughter first?" Ginny asked.

Brett laughed. "Hopefully, they'll teach her how to cook. One thing is for sure—she'll be the most spoiled little girl in Three Trees. But, why worry now? We have a long time to work all this out."

"I don't know," Ginny said, "it seems like the last seven months went by pretty quickly."

Brett slowly sat up, putting his back to Ginny. He sniffed lightly as he ran his hands across his eyes. After a moment he cleared his throat. His voice was rougher when he asked, "Do you have something to tell me, Dove?"

"Yes," she answered, "I think Daniel would be a good name for our first son."

"That was my father's name."

"I know."

Brett turned and placed his hand over Ginny's small belly. "What if it's a girl?"

"We have the next seven months to decide."

A word about the author...

Sandra Dailey is an avid reader and lifelong storyteller. She caught the writing bug after winning a short story contest. *The Chief's Proposal* is her first published work, but she has many more stories to tell.

Sandra currently lives with her husband in north Florida.

You can contact her at:

sandradailey.author@gmail.com

www.sandradailey.com

www.sandradailey.blogspot.com